Once Upon
a Cowboy

LACY WILLIAMS

THE COWBOY FAIRYTALES SERIES

ONCE UPON A COWBOY

CHAPTER ONE

Early February

Just keep smiling.

Princess Alessandra, second in line for the throne of Glorvaird, meandered through the crush of bodies as the Who's-Who of New York City society mingled on the sidewalk outside a ritzy hotel. Inside the ballroom would be even worse, stuffy with the heat of so many people. The icy air chilled her skin where the slinky dress she wore didn't cover nearly enough beneath her designer coat, but inside she'd be grateful to shed her outerwear.

She detested events like these. But her royal duty demanded her presence. Her sister, the crown princess, had tasked her with forging alliances with two powerful dignitaries, which she would attempt when she could get inside. Two hours, and she could return to her own hotel, several blocks away. And rid herself of the awful, pinching heels her stylist had provided.

Paparazzi snapped pictures from behind a cordoned-off line, the flashes from their cameras whisking her to the present and out of her thoughts. Hired security milled around, looking bored. After years of being in the public eye, she was used to the presence of both.

It didn't mean the press weren't as annoying as gnats, constantly buzzing in her ear.

One misstep, one faux pas, could follow her around on the Internet for a year.

She smoothed her skirt unobtrusively and kept the smile fixed on her face.

A hand on her elbow made her pause amidst the crowd.

Her bodyguard. Tim was dark-haired and fair-complected, bulky, and more than a head taller than she. He usually faded into the background.

The fact that he'd moved in close had her pulse speeding.

"What's—" *wrong?*

She didn't get both words out before a *pop* echoed above the rumble of the crowd.

Tim's body jerked.

He fell into her. Knocked her off the precarious heels. They tumbled together. Her elbow scraped against the pavement.

The crowd rumbled. Feet shuffled in the

periphery as the other high society types didn't seem to know whether to move closer or farther away.

Alessandra struggled to separate herself from Tim, but he weighed close to a hundred pounds more than she did, and his body was heavy and unmoving. Her coat had fallen open when he'd landed atop her, and they seemed to be tangled together.

Why wasn't he moving?

"Stay—down," he gasped.

Someone screamed.

And she realized the hot, sticky substance that covered her hand where she'd tried to push him off was blood. *His* blood.

"Tim!"

Blind panic added strength to her scrambling, and at last she was able to push him off. He rolled to his back, his suit coat falling open to reveal his white shirt stained red.

"Someone—" She looked up at the blur of faces surrounding her. There was no one she recognized.

She pressed her hands to Tim's chest to try and stop the flow of blood, but more seeped up between her fingers. *No!*

"Please, is there a doctor?" she called out. In the cacophony of voices, she couldn't make out a distinct answer. "Can someone call for help?"

But as she looked down on the man bleeding out

beneath her hands, she realized it was too late. Tim's eyes had gone glassy and unfocused.

He was gone.

Someone had shot him.

He'd died protecting *her.*

Her fright didn't recede as she glanced at the faces surrounding her. Some sympathetic. Some crying, panicking now that they realized the nightmare was real. Two of the hired policemen edged through the crowd and knelt beside her.

They provided scant cover.

Was someone waiting to take another shot? A sniper? A killer in the crowd?

If she stood, would another bullet find her? Would she collapse beside Tim, her life dripping out onto the New York sidewalk?

She'd stayed crouched beside the man who'd given everything to protect her, shielded by the police who hovered near. People everywhere. Noises. The scent of blood.

She'd never felt so alone.

One thing was clear. She had to get away.

Far, far away.

~ * ~

Gideon Hale winced as he stepped off the somewhat

sheltered back porch and into the biting February wind. He'd already waved Apollo, a German Shepherd Dog, back inside to his bed in the mudroom. No use in both of them freezing their guts out here tonight.

It was after ten and the other cowhands were abed. Not him.

At least it wasn't snowing. Or sleeting. For now. The north Texas weather could change quickly, and often did.

He left the ranch house behind, his booted strides quickly eating up the distance across the yard. The moon shone above the row of elms that lined the gravel drive, casting eerie shadows. By rote, his eyes scanned for anything out of place. Until he shook himself out of it.

This wasn't Afghanistan. Or any of the top-secret locations he'd traveled to.

By the time he hit the barn, his hands were chilled inside his leather gloves. He slipped through the double doors and pulled them closed behind him.

The barn was split into two sections. One enclosed, one open to the elements. It provided shelter to the Angus cows that were his family's livelihood, allowing the mamas and babies free access to the paddock beyond.

He'd brought in two prospective mamas from the

larger, western field earlier in the day, suspecting they were close to giving birth.

This was a critical time of year for the Triple-H. Calving season. The next few weeks would determine how much of a profit they'd make this year. His family was counting on him.

And he knew it was Mother Nature, not a conscious choice, but it seemed as if the animals always gave birth on the most bitter nights of the year.

When he checked on the soon-to-be mamas, they were resting peacefully. No signs of agitation, no sign that they were close to giving birth.

Which made him suspicious. Running a herd of fifteen-hundred, they rarely went a day this time of year without several births.

So he bundled his work coat tighter around himself and went out the back of the barn, rounding the side of the structure to where the UTV was parked. It didn't want to crank, probably because of the bitter temperatures. He prayed it wasn't the battery, prayed he wouldn't get stranded out in the fields on a night like this and have to walk home.

The UTV started, and he threw it in gear, bumping his way out of the barnyard and into the field behind. The vehicle had a windshield but little else to shelter him from the open air, and he was frozen through by the time he reached the paddock where the rest of the mamas and expecting mamas were kept.

Sometimes, on nights like this, he wished he was back on the Teams. It had been blisteringly hot during their last covert mission in a place he wasn't supposed to talk about, and he'd lost several pounds of water weight. Two years ago, he'd been an integral part of the close-knit team. Had been armed and lying on his stomach on the sand next to Cash, too close to the Tangoes to whisper a joke or two, separated from the rest of their team by a few hundred yards as they waited for the order to infiltrate.

It hadn't been comfortable. And it wasn't the adrenaline rush that he missed now.

It was the camaraderie. Those guys knew him. They were like brothers.

Gideon had blown his knee out on that mission, injured himself so badly that he wasn't fit for duty anymore. And while he'd been in the hospital, his stepdad had died. Which meant his little brother and sister had needed him to run the Triple H.

So here he was. Missing his SEAL family and freezing his toes off on what might be a wild goose chase. He gritted his teeth against the thoughts. Shook them off. What he had been didn't matter now. His place was here.

He located the herd, tucked in a shallow gully. Between the UTV headlights and the fog lights rigged on the roof, he started counting.

One cow was missing. Or maybe he'd counted wrong.

Thoughts of his warm bed had him closing his eyes for a split second. Then, with a groan, he reversed the UTV and started making another pass. Hopeful he'd been wrong.

But a second count didn't turn up the cow. Gideon had worked the herd long enough to know their markings and ear tag numbers and realized this was one of the few heifers who'd been bred. This would be her first delivery.

She'd probably be fine. Cows had been giving birth since the beginning of time, right?

But the bitter cold and the fact that sometimes cows that hadn't delivered a baby before got into trouble had him stubbornly refusing to give up. A lost cow was lost money. More when you considered the calf too. His family depended on the Triple H's income. After what Carrie had been through, she deserved for him to give it his all, even if it wasn't what he dreamed about in the dark of night.

He'd take one last pass through the pasture and see if he couldn't find the heifer.

Maybe he'd get back to bed before one. If he was lucky.

CHAPTER TWO

Gideon didn't make it to bed at all.

By the time he'd found her, the cow had been in labor and was very distressed. There'd been blood, and she'd been down. He'd had no way to get her back to the warm barn, so he'd stripped out of his shirt and done what he could to assist the birth.

Turned out there was a reason she'd been in trouble. She'd given birth to twins. With the mama so weak—although she'd quickly gotten to her feet—and two calves shivering and covered in fluid, he'd known he had to get them back to the barn.

Which was a trial-and-a-half, because the mama had turned protective, fast.

It'd been nearly four when he'd finally stumbled into the farmhouse. Only to find Nate, the foreman, scrambling two dozen eggs for the rest of the hands. He'd spent a half hour discussing the day's agenda and stressing the need for Nate to send one of the hands out to check for more newborn babies in the field.

If it'd been any other day, he might've caught a combat nap, but his brother Matt was flying in on an early-morning flight, and the website showed it was on-time, which left Gideon only time for a quick shower.

Now, after a two-and-a-half hour drive to Dallas and sitting an hour in traffic, he waited in the baggage claim for his little bro.

Little.

Matt was active duty Air Force and on leave from his tour overseas. Gideon was proud of him.

And maybe a bit jealous too.

His bum knee *panged* in sympathy, and he shifted his feet, trying to alleviate some of the pressure. His eyes flicked to a TV angled from the ceiling. It was hard to hear in the echoing cavern of the luggage claim, but he caught the words "assassination attempt," and he zoned in. Apparently some European princess had gone missing in New York City. He wondered if any military personnel would be called in to help, or if the Feds were handling it.

And then he didn't have time to wonder anymore, because passengers started trickling down the escalators. Then came a flood, complete with a large family of jostling teenaged boys and a smaller family with a squalling baby and a toddler clinging to mom's pant leg. Dad pushed an overloaded stroller and looked like he wanted to be anywhere else.

And there was Matt, his fatigues and crew cut instantly recognizable among the civilian clothing surrounding him. He looked exhausted and stressed, lines fanning from the corners of his eyes. When he caught sight of Gideon, he smiled, but it was rough.

Gideon's stomach clamped into a tight ball. Something was wrong. He watched his brother's approach closely but couldn't see any signs of injury.

Then Matt was beside him.

"Hey, man." He wasn't ashamed to pull his brother into a back-slapping hug. "Good to see you." And it was. Now that he was on the other side of the deployment, he'd realized how much worry he'd put his family through while he'd been off on missions.

They both backed off to a respectable, manly distance. "You're looking pasty, old man," Matt said.

"Long night." Gideon shoved the Stetson back on his forehead. "Little heifer gave birth to twins out in the field."

Matt squinted. "And you had to help?"

Gideon shrugged. She'd been in pretty bad situation when he'd arrived on the scene, with the first calf twisted up in the womb. "They survived the night."

"How's Carrie and the little booger?" Matt asked

as they turned to follow the crowd.

"They're fine. Can't wait to see you at dinner tonight."

They moved closer to the carousel, which now spun. Luggage appeared in a slow trickle. When Matt grabbed his government-issued duffel, Gideon couldn't help looking over his brother again. Was Matt limping slightly? He couldn't be sure. His brother was saying all the right things, but something was off.

Gideon made his brother hand over the duffel—which Matt did with only a minimum of stink-eye—and slung it over his shoulder as he led the way to the parking garage.

"You hungry? Figured we could stop somewhere on the way back to the Triple H."

Matt shifted his nearer shoulder, and Gideon resisted the urge to narrow his eyes. Dislocated? Or was Gideon just being paranoid? Trying to see the worries that plagued him because he could guess what his brother had walked into over there?

"Sure, I could eat."

That was a good sign, at least.

They reached the right level in the parking garage and approached the truck. Gideon stowed Matt's duffel in the truck bed, where it landed next to the blue tarp he'd thrown over the tools he'd used two days ago to repair a section of broken fencing in one of the pastures. He'd meant to unload the tools in the barn yesterday but had never gotten around to it.

He was glad to hop in the truck and crank the heater. He rubbed his chapped hands together. If anything, it had gotten colder in the night, although he hadn't heard about a front moving through.

He felt the shift in the cargo as he backed out of the parking space and kicked the truck into *Drive*. Hadn't realized he'd used that many tools.

Matt slouched in his seat, long legs eating up the space beneath the dash.

"How long is your leave?"

"Three weeks. Maybe a month." He grunted. "Why, you need another hand for the spring cutting?"

Gideon grinned. Castrating bull calves, turning them into steers, had been his brother's least favorite task on the ranch during their growing up years. "If you're going to be a sissy about it, I'm sure the hands and I can handle it without you."

Matt leaned his head against the seat-back. "Trey still hanging around? Still mooning over Carrie?"

"I don't know about mooning. We've still got the same guys working for us. Nate, Brian, Trey, Dan, Chase. If cattle prices stay up, we'll make enough from the summer sale to buy out old man Cameron.

Maybe add another hundred head."

Matt grunted again. He'd worked the ranch, same as Gideon, and left as soon as he was of age. Same as Gideon. Neither one of them had wanted to stay on and work the ranch long-term. Only now Gideon was back, running the ranch for their family. Trying not to chafe under the small-town life.

Carrie needed him. He owed her.

"Think *Gerry's* will be too busy for breakfast?" Matt asked.

The mom-and-pop diner was halfway home, not too far off the interstate, and a popular eatery in three counties. Mama G, the proprietress, served a mean omelet.

"Might be too busy if I hadn't called Mama G on my way down and told her you were back home for awhile. She's reserving a table for you, soldier-boy."

Matt grinned, but there was something behind the smile that Gideon couldn't read, not when he needed to keep his eyes on the interstate traffic.

Over an hour later, they exited I-30. It'd be another fifteen minutes of two-lane highway to *Gerry's*. They'd covered all the small talk Gideon could stand in his exhausted state and fallen into a comfortable silence. It'd always been like that growing up. They'd understood each other, sometimes hadn't needed words.

A thump from the truck bed had Gideon glancing in the rearview mirror, then reaching up to tug the mirror down so he could see. He hadn't taken the last turn fast enough for the tools and duffel to shift. Not that much.

Was something moving back there? He hadn't seen any kind of bird come out of the sky. He'd checked that Apollo hadn't hopped up in the truck bed before he'd left the house this morning at oh-dark-hundred.

Matt had been staring out the window, but now came alert, sitting up straight. "What's the matter?" He twisted in his seat, glancing out the back window, then back at Gideon.

"Something moved in the back."

He felt Matt's skeptical stare. "Like what?"

Gideon shrugged, shifting his neck side to side. He'd been sitting in the truck for too long this morning after a long night, and his muscles were tight. "Something."

He spotted a turnout off the two-lane state highway and put on his blinker.

"Seriously?"

He glanced at his brother, brows raised. "You're that hungry for Mama G's cooking? Can't wait two minutes for me to tie down my tools?"

Matt just frowned.

Gideon stopped with a crunch of the tires on dirt and threw the truck into Park. "Just give me a minute."

Of course Matt followed him out of the truck.

He'd left it idling, but something rustled beneath the tarp even above the engine noise. Glancing at Matt over the truck bed, he reached in and rolled back the tarp to find a white-faced woman huddled beneath.

~ * ~

Alessandra was frozen through. She couldn't feel her fingers or toes, and her teeth had stopped chattering an hour ago. She'd never been so cold her teeth ceased chattering. The irony of escaping an assassin only to die of hypothermia.

She barely registered that the truck had stopped before the darkness of her covering lifted and she came face-to-face with a grizzly bear. With a jolt she realized it was a man, but with a dark, shaggy beard covering his face and long hair that fell into his eyes, he might as well have been a bear. The look in his intense, dark eyes said he'd kill her.

"Who are you?" he growled.

She tried to answer, but her lips wouldn't form words.

"She's half-frozen," said another voice. Her neck twinged when she tried to turn her head, and she strained her eyes to the opposite side of the truck bed to see another man, this one clean cut and in a military uniform, although he shared the same dark eyes as the first. Related?

Her heart pounded with fear, but she still couldn't make her muscles move. She had no strength left, not after running for thirty-six hours. She'd passed through six airports, spent most of that time hiding in restrooms and freaking out over every glance another passenger sent her way.

The first man—the grizzly bear—grunted and reached for her. She was used to everyone carefully staying out of her personal space, but she couldn't form a protest when his hand clamped around her upper arm. He tugged, and she slid across the slippery metal truck bed.

And then he hauled her bodily over the side, lifting her easily, as if she were a bag of Glorvaird apples or one of the tools that had been poking her beneath the plastic tarp.

Military-man stayed on his side of the truck.

Her legs wobbled, but she didn't fall when he set her on her feet.

Who where they? Did they mean her harm?

"L-let g-go of me." There. She'd gotten the words

out, and even with the wobble, she'd sounded almost imperial.

The grizzly bear did let go, and she had to clutch the side of the pickup and lock her knees to keep from tumbling to the ground.

She didn't like the way he looked her up and down. Not the way she was used to men looking at her. Usually they were assessing her figure, not her threat level.

She wasn't the threat. He was!

"Who are you?" he demanded. "Why were you stowed away in my truck?"

She stalled, looking away from the bear's narrow-eyed gaze and over his shoulder instead.

She'd hoped to escape the airport without being tracked by surveillance cameras, hoped that when the truck stopped, she'd be able to unobtrusively get out without anyone being the wiser.

She'd failed.

And it appeared she'd hitched a ride to the middle of nowhere. They'd stopped along a stretch of lonely two-lane road. Fields of red-brown dirt extended to the horizon in both directions. There was nothing else within eyesight. Just the two men and the truck.

No escape.

She should be worried, but right now, she felt only the same numbness that had stolen over her yesterday.

"How'd you get in my truck?" he demanded. His eyes glittered with what she assumed was anger.

"I c-climbed in. I n-needed to get o-out of the airport w-without being seen." She'd snuck down the escalators to the parking garage, hiding in a large group that seemed to be coming off a mission trip, judging by their colorful backpacks with patches sewn on. In the parking garage, the group had loaded up into two large vans, and she'd been left alone, creeping between vehicles and not sure what to do next.

Then, a scary-looking man with a shaved head had come off the elevator, and she'd panicked anew. Had he tracked her here from New York?

She'd seen the beat-up truck and the plastic blanket inside the bed and quickly jumped in and covered herself up. It could barely be called a plan. It evidently hadn't been a good one.

She was finding she wasn't very good at taking care of herself. Although at least when she'd been running, she hadn't had time to think about...

The bear must've said something else that she'd missed, lost in her thoughts. She was getting kind of foggy. She still wore the evening dress and long coat she'd had on for the benefit two evenings ago. The clothes were impractical and had done nothing to keep her warm, exposed as she was in the back of the truck.

"Gideon, get her in the truck."

The bear—Gideon—growled at the other man. Maybe he really was part-animal.

"Does she look dangerous?"

Gideon the Bear assessed her again with a long up-and-down glance. He muttered something under his breath and moved toward her, gripped her upper arm.

She tried to pull away. Too weak. He towed her to the cab, yanked open the door with his opposite hand, and practically shoved her inside.

The other man, the soldier, was getting in from the passenger side. "You need some help?" he asked, as she struggled to make her icy muscles move enough to slide in the truck.

She shook her head slightly.

There was no way to ignore the presence of Gideon the Bear behind her, and she soon found herself squished between the two broad-shouldered men. The soldier reached across and turned the knob for the heater. It was already much warmer, just being inside the truck, but the extra heat bled through her skin and into her extremities. And it felt so good.

Until her skin started to prickle. And then it didn't

feel good at all.

~ * ~

Gideon shared a look with Matt above the blonde's head as she began to shiver violently.

She was putting on a brave face, but he knew what it felt like to be so close to hypothermia—he'd been close once, on his very first mission with the teams.

When your body started warming up, it felt like tiny knives pricking all over your skin. It hurt.

Judging from the fancy dress and coat—was she even wearing stockings?—he guessed she had exposure, though the skin he could see wasn't the awful grayish-white that would indicate frostbite, or he'd be driving her to the nearest hospital.

He didn't think Matt's motives for getting her in the truck were entirely altruistic. His brother had to have known that the heat would be painful for her. No, Matt knew that now was the time to get some information out of her.

"Who are you?" Gideon asked again.

She glanced at him askance. "N-no one." Her teeth were chattering now, which he guessed was a good sign.

Matt stared at the woman.

Gideon could admit she was attractive. Striking,

with her pale blue eyes and long blonde hair. She'd looked so frightened when he'd pulled back the tarp. Like a waif in need of rescuing.

Which just raised his suspicions higher. Something was really wrong here.

Why had she targeted *his* truck?

"What's your name?" Gideon pressed. "What're you running from?" Because it was obvious she was running from something. The evening gown and coat stunk of money. And those shoes... they were impractical, skinny heels and strappy—you'd break your ankle trying to make a quick getaway. Even the faint whiff of perfume she wore smelled of money.

And for a moment when he'd pulled her out of the truck, her coat had fallen open, and he'd thought he'd seen a dark stain inside. Dried blood?

Everything about her was setting off warning bells in his head.

And then Matt raised his eyes to meet Gideon's gaze above her head again, and this time he shook his head slightly.

Gideon shook his head right back. Matt might be a trained soldier, but Gideon was an operator and trusted his instincts. He didn't know what his little brother was thinking. Coddling her?

Matt didn't back down. *I know who she is*, he mouthed above her head.

What—how?

"Can you—take me somewhere with a telephone?" the woman asked.

"We aren't going anywhere until you give me some answers."

Matt frowned at him.

She looked past him, to the door.

Let her try.

She was trapped between the two of them. No way would a lightweight like her be able to get past a former SEAL and a soldier. And anyway, if she got out of the truck, where would she go? Only one stock-hauling semi had passed them since they'd pulled over. No way was she walking far in those shoes.

"You promised me *Gerry's*," Matt reminded him.

Gideon resisted the urge to roll his eyes. How could his brother be slave to his stomach right now? The fact that there had been a woman hiding in the back of his truck had derailed their breakfast plans.

"Let's take her with us," Matt continued, as if Gideon had already agreed. "We can figure out what to do from there."

No way.

Matt must've seen his refusal in the set of his jaw. He mouthed, *trust me.*

Gideon knew his little brother probably meant

well, but Gideon was driving. He was in charge here.

But judging by the stubborn set of the woman's chin, she wasn't giving answers anytime soon. Could Matt really know who she was?

Gideon rested one wrist over the steering wheel and glanced at the land surrounding him. There was nothing here. They had another ten miles to go before they reached the small town where *Gerry's* was located.

What was he going to do, leave her to hitchhike? He might be suspicious, but he wasn't cruel.

No way was a cab or Uber driver from the city driving all the way out to *Gerry's* to pick her up, but if they left her with a hundred bucks, it didn't count as abandoning her, did it?

What other choice did they have? It's not like he'd invited her to hitch a ride in his truck.

"Fine." He put the truck in gear and hit the gas, pulling back onto the two-lane.

Matt yanked his phone from one of his cargo pockets and played with it. Seriously, his text couldn't wait until they got this mess figured out?

The woman remained silent, rocking slightly back and forth, though her shivers had lessened.

A few minutes later, they pulled in front of *Gerry's* and found a lucky parking spot at the back of the lot—lucky because they didn't have to park in the overflow lot across the street. The sleepy little town was mostly quiet, no traffic coming down Main Street, even though *Gerry's* lot was full. The feed store two doors down also boasted a few cars in the lot, but the church and bank across the street seemed virtually empty.

He got out, motioning for the woman to follow him. "C'mon."

He saw her glance around as she slid from the truck until her feet touched the ground.

"Don't even think about it." He took her upper arm, ensuring she wouldn't try to bolt. What had her so flighty?

"I'll thank you not to put your hands on me." Her voice wasn't wobbling anymore, and that tilt of her chin... was she seriously trying to order him around?

"When I start getting some answers, we can negotiate."

Matt shot him a look as he joined them in front of the truck, sandwiching the woman between them.

Inside, the restaurant was bustling. Mama G, slightly overweight and in her fifties, must've been watching for them, because she was out from behind the counter before the bell above the door had quit ringing, her arms thrown around Matt in an exuberant hug.

Several good 'ol boys took up seats at the

counter—probably a few of them Vets. They started clapping, and soon the restaurant erupted in applause and "welcome homes," for his brother. Matt deserved it, even if they didn't know most of these folks.

And Gideon used the distraction to tow the woman to the booth against the wall with a small, handwritten *Reserved* card sitting on its edge.

The woman glared at him, but he was much bigger than she was, and she allowed herself to be nudged into one side of the booth.

He followed her in, blocking her way out.

The applause died out, and Matt approached, accepting several backslaps on his way. He slid into the opposite side of the booth and handed Gideon his phone.

The screen was lit with a picture that did look sort of like the woman sitting regally beside him, her back straight as a poker. Sort of. The phone picture showed a beautiful young woman with perfectly-styled hair and too much makeup smiling at the camera. The woman beside him looked bedraggled, her hair limp, her face pale. Definitely her.

She glared at him, and he glanced back at the phone. Read the photo caption. *Princess Alessandra of Glorvaird* at some fancy-pants reception last year.

A princess?

Suddenly, he remembered the newscast he'd caught only seconds of in the airport. This was the princess who'd been shot at in New York? Whose bodyguard had died?

How in the heck had she ended up here?

LACY WILLIAMS

CHAPTER THREE

Alessandra watched in horror as Gideon the Bear glanced at the phone's screen. Her own picture looked back at her.

Her heart beat in her throat, threatening to choke her.

Any chance at anonymity she'd had was gone.

The question remained: what would they do now? The two strangers could hold her for ransom. Abandon her.

But the compassionate glance that the soldier sent her... Somehow, she knew the brother in military garb was on her side. Would he help her?

Gideon the Bear's head came up slowly. While he'd been suspicious and surly before, something clicked inside him as quickly as his posture changed. Where he'd been tense, now his shoulders had straightened, something tight and controlled in his actions.

"I guess you've had a hard couple of days, haven't

you?" Military-man asked.

At his words, unbidden tears filled her eyes.

Tim.

She'd tried to keep him from her thoughts. but every time she closed her eyes or started to drift off, images of his blood flowing up between her fingers played behind her eyes. He was dead.

She blinked at the images now, working to erase them.

Gideon the Bear shifted closer to her—close enough for their thighs to brush—and she tensed.

"Easy," the soldier said, his voice a low rumble that barely carried across the table. He tilted his head, and she followed his glance to a young woman wearing an apron over her T-shirt and jeans, rapidly approaching their table.

Gideon's arm stretched across the back of the booth. Not quite touching, but close enough that she felt the heat radiating from him.

She wasn't used to the closeness, to someone else being in her space, and she wanted to curl into a ball in the corner of the booth, regardless of the soldier's assurance.

"Pull your coat closed," the Bear murmured, head tilted toward her, as if they were having an intimate conversation. "It stands out, but not as bad as your dress underneath."

She didn't have to look around to know it was true. On the way in, she'd seen the older men in overalls and worn flannel shirts, the young mother with her brood in stained discount-store clothing.

She stuck out like a sore thumb.

She might not trust Gideon the Bear, but she could admit he was right.

She pulled her coat closed and crossed her arms just as the waitress reached their table.

"So you're back." It was said to the soldier with a smile, but Alessandra had grown up around politicians, dignitaries and other royals, and she easily read the tension behind the woman's expression.

"So I am." The soldier's return smile was more genuine, but still, an something underlying remained. "Life treating you right, Katie?"

"Just dandy." Only the words rang somehow false. Katie raised her order pad and pencil. "What can I get you?" While at first she'd only seemed to have eyes for the soldier, now her gaze widened to encompass Alessandra and Gideon as well.

Alessandra wanted to shrink beneath the table. If the two men had recognized her so easily, just how quickly would someone else discover her identity?

"Coffees all around," the soldier said easily. "And three of the house specials. Gideon said his girl has been begging him to bring her here for weeks.

Right?"

Gideon's *what?*

Alessandra forced a trembling smile when the waitress's gaze darted back to her. She tried not to lean quite so far away from the hulking man at her side.

The man beside her didn't seem happy with the soldier's explanation either. She could see a muscle ticking beneath his eye.

Thankfully, the waitress didn't comment, only scratched something on her order pad before she turned away. A man in a worn ball cap with a green logo above the bill waved her down before she'd gone two steps.

"Way to act natural," the soldier scoffed.

"That was probably the worst thing you could've said," the Bear returned, leaning forward slightly, over the table. "If she wants to avoid people scrutinizing her. Everyone around here knows I haven't dated in"—his furious whisper broke off as he glanced at her briefly—"a long time."

The soldier shrugged, a smirk playing around the edges of his mouth. "It's about time," he said. "You're not getting any younger."

Gideon grunted.

The waitress reappeared at Gideon's elbow, efficiently setting three cups of coffee on the table, along with a small open carafe of creamer. "Sugar's on the table." She scurried away to buss a table that had just emptied.

The soldier's gaze stayed with Katie for longer than was really necessary.

Gideon scooted Alessandra's mug closer, and she wrapped her hands around it, grateful for the warmth that bled into her still-chilled body. He nudged the creamer her way, and she took it too.

"Thank you," she murmured.

"Ah, so you can talk."

She looked up sharply at his words. His dark eyes glittered, but it was almost impossible to read his expression behind the heavy, shaggy beard.

"Gid," the soldier chided. He sent an apologetic look to her. "I think we've got off on the wrong foot. I'm Matt Hale. Gideon is my big brother. My grumpy big brother. And you're—"

"Allie," Gideon interrupted. He didn't glance around furtively or do anything that might've brought attention to them, but he practically skewered his brother with a dark-eyed gaze. "It's better if you don't call her anything else."

Allie. She experienced a flash of memory from her childhood, when she'd wanted to be "just Allie," and live with the head housekeeper.

She blinked the memory away. She hadn't thought

about that in years.

Had the shock of her ordeal caught up with her?

She let out a shaky breath. "If you recognized me," she nodded to Matt, "what's to stop someone else from doing so as well?" She sipped her doctored coffee, but the warmth didn't reach all the way inside, where she'd frozen solid when Tim had stepped in front of that bullet for her.

Matt smiled, an easy smile. Now that there was no sign of their waitress, his body language relaxed. He slouched in the bench seat, clearly at ease. "I spent all day yesterday in airports. They must've replayed the same news coverage every hour. But around here... most of the folks don't get cable or pay much attention to national news coverage. They maybe got a blip on the local nightly news."

She glanced at Gideon, who wasn't at all relaxed like his brother. But he nodded, confirming Matt's words.

"No one around here would expect to meet a"— he waved his hand her way—"someone like you. People see what they want to see."

Their confidence was something of a relief, but it didn't help with her current predicament.

"I'm U.S. Air Force," Matt said. "And Gideon is a former Navy SEAL. You might not have handpicked his truck before you climbed into it, but you've found two guys who are willing and able to help you."

Gideon mumbled something beneath his breath. He didn't seem happy to be sitting next to her.

Well, that made two of them.

The waitress made another appearance, this time delivering three steaming plates of omelets, bacon, sausage and toast.

Matt had already shoveled two bites into his mouth before the waitress had walked away.

The food smells, salty and meaty and hot, rose to Alessandra's nose. She had to be hungry.

But her body's response was off.

Alessandra stared down at her plate, wondering if she'd be able to eat at all. Yesterday, she'd been so focused on getting away from New York City, getting somewhere safe, that she had barely paid attention to her body's needs. When she'd bought a health bar from a vending machine in one of the airports she'd bounced around, she'd barely been able to stomach it, still reeling, grieving over Tim.

But now...her stomach gave an audible growl.

Matt seemed oblivious, his eyes closed as he savored the food.

But Gideon had to have heard it. He shifted slightly in the seat, his knee bumping hers in their close proximity. "It gets easier," he said in a low voice.

She glanced at him briefly, unsure how to take his meaning.

"To go on."

It didn't seem fair. She could go on eating. Go on living. When Tim would never have the chance.

But she also didn't have a choice. She had a duty to her family. To her father. To her people.

She picked up a strip of bacon and bit into it. Salty, greasy goodness exploded over her tongue. Tears pricked her eyes at both the rightness and the wrongness of being able to enjoy it.

Thankfully, both men pretended not to notice as she raised her paper napkin to her face and dabbed at her tears.

A few moments passed in silence as the three of them ate.

"What happened after you left the—the scene of the shooting?" Gideon asked, his own fork clinking against his plate.

"Gid," Matt admonished through a mouthful of food.

"If she wants our help, we need to know what's going on. Have all the facts."

She hadn't said whether she would accept their help. Her gut told her she could trust the two men, but she didn't know whether she could risk putting someone else in danger. If what happened in New

York had truly been an assassination attempt, what would keep the assassin from tracking her down?

She also didn't have any other choices, because after she'd maxed out the cash allowance on her cards back at the airport in Boston, she'd ditched her purse, cards and identification and everything, too afraid someone could track her movements.

"The police took me into a private room in the hotel," she said softly. She couldn't look at them, kept her gaze focused on her plate. "I made a phone call to the pal—to my sister." She'd almost blurted out that she'd called the *palace*. How stupid could she be? She was terrible at subterfuge. "There was—something was going on there as well."

The two men seemed to take her meaning without her having to explain everything—at least not for now. Gideon seemed the kind of person who left no secret unexplored. Pushy as he was.

She couldn't exactly say *bomb* aloud without risking someone overhearing and making the connection.

A bomb had been set off at the palace gates, nearly hitting a limousine that carried her younger sister, Mia. Just thinking about it made any remaining appetite vanish. Alessandra pushed her plate slightly away.

Her older sister Eloise had assured her that she and Mia and their father were fine, that most of the staff had been unharmed, but that they were on lockdown.

"I was told to go underground," she whispered. "Without Tim, I...did the best I could."

The visit to New York was only to last a few days, and the palace security team had deemed it completely safe. Tim had been her only guard.

How wrong they'd been.

Matt nodded, eyes sympathetic. She hesitated to turn her head and take in Gideon's expression. When she finally looked, his eyes were narrowed, assessing. Did he think she was *lying?*

"Any idea who wants—who would do something like this?"

She'd followed his first sentence before he'd cut himself off. *Any idea who wants you dead?*

"My aunt."

An hour and a half later, Gideon paced in the farmhouse kitchen, feeling caged.

He wanted to do more than pace. He wanted to put his fist through something.

He couldn't believe he'd agreed to Matt's farfetched plan. *Hide a princess on the Triple H?*

Matt had been right when he'd said they couldn't

leave the princess to her own devices. She'd lucked out when she'd jumped in the back of his truck, finding help instead of someone who would do her harm. It was obvious she had no idea how to survive on her own. She hadn't even taken the time to purchase some cheap, touristy clothes in one of the airport shops, which might've given her some anonymity while she'd traveled. She'd still been wearing the slinky evening dress and heels she'd worn at the time of the shooting!

It would've been easy for Gideon to track her, if that had been his assignment.

He could only hope and pray that whoever had come after her in New York was a moron, or that their assignment had been to scare her off, not kill her.

He wanted answers from her so-called security team. He'd questioned her in-depth in the truck on the ride here, but she'd claimed they'd deemed her trip safe, kept the security light.

There could be someone on the inside. It was possible. That was one explanation for letting as assassin get so close to her.

Or else they were idiots.

He might be one too, because if someone was still after her, he'd just put his own family in danger. And that was something he couldn't live with.

With calving season upon them, he didn't have time to babysit a spoiled, rich princess who undoubtedly was used to a large staff catering to her every whim. He'd already reached out to one of his old SEAL teammates, Cash, asked for information about the investigation behind the shooting and bombing—he'd had to pry that out of her too—and gave him a heads up as to the princess's location. The other man had advised Gideon to lay low, keep her hidden.

This was a huge mistake. Gideon knew it, but he hadn't been able to talk Matt out of it or think of another solution on the fly. And looking down on the princess's wide, frightened eyes, he hadn't been able to tell her *no*, either.

He'd been shocked to feel compassion flare when she'd become visibly upset over the death of her bodyguard. That she'd felt such deep emotion over the loss of someone she employed made her seem...human. Almost.

He heard a tread on the stairs and stopped pacing. Faced the mission head-on, hands at his sides.

Her feet came into view first—bare—as she descended the steps from the second floor. Then a slender pair of legs encased in jeans. They were borrowed from a stash of clothes his sister had left behind and fit a little too snugly in the hips. A chambray work shirt over a faded T-shirt completed the outfit. With her hair pulled back in a braid behind her head, she looked the part of a working cowgirl.

He knew how badly appearances could deceive.

As she landed on the second-to-last step, her gaze lifted and their eyes met. Something in the soft blue depths hit him square in the chest.

It was uncomfortable. And he didn't like it. He flicked his gaze away, instead staring just over her right shoulder.

"You'll want to stay in the house," he said, voice a bit more gruff than he'd intended. "There's livestock roaming every pasture, and you're likely to get stepped on or scare them—and most of them are calving right now."

She nodded slowly.

He went on. "We're having supper tonight to celebrate my brother's leave—time off. You can stay out of sight, if you want. Or you can come down, meet all the hands. And my sister, Carrie."

She pressed her palms together, interlocking her fingers just in front of her midsection. A picture of calm. But he caught the slight tremble of her hands. "Is there anything I can do to help?"

He didn't figure someone who got waited on hand-and-foot knew her way around a kitchen, so the offer sounded pretty weak to him. "Nope. Just lay low."

He needed to get back out to the barn, get Dan on the radio and make sure the boys were making progress fencing off the far south pasture, but there was one more thing.

He approached the princess, bristling internally when she tensed. He knew she must be having a rough time of it, but he'd opened his home to her, offered his protection. Not something he did lightly. The least she could do was not flinch when he came near.

"Here," he gruffed. He held out his smartphone.

She just stared at him.

Finally, impatient, he waggled it. "Take it," he ordered. "It's mine. For emergencies. I've got a burner phone I can use for now. I've programmed numbers for me and Matt at the top of the contacts. I'd hold off calling or emailing your family for now— it's possible a hacker could intercept the signal and track where you are. Possible, not likely," he amended when her face paled.

She took the phone from him, her fingers a cool brush against his palm. "Thank you." She looked him directly, which bought her a modicum of respect. "For everything. I know I'm putting you out, and I hope to give you a more official thank you when I can get back to—to the palace."

He didn't need her thanks, but he nodded anyway. "I've got work to do."

~ * ~

Alessandra stood in the hallway after Gideon the Bear had stalked past her and out through what appeared to be a mudroom, judging by the number of dirty boots piled on a rug next to the back door.

She should really stop thinking of him that way. He might look like a bear, might snarl and snuffle and grunt like one, but he'd shown her kindness by offering his home. Reluctant though the offer might have been.

She turned the phone over in her hands, at a loss.

Normally, every moment of her day was scheduled. Events for charities the palace supported. Keynote speeches. Time spent being updated on current events across the globe. Except for the scant, early-morning hours where she snuck "below-stairs," she rarely had time to herself.

Thus, the loss. She didn't know what to do with herself.

She turned a slow circle, taking in her surroundings. When they'd arrived, Matt had taken a phone call and wandered off toward the big, red barn that was situated on a slight hill above the house.

Gideon had brought her inside and given her the change of clothes, but it was obvious he'd been in a hurry to get back to his work. She'd barely looked around when she'd come inside.

At the foot of the stairs, she stood in what appeared to be the heart of the home. The staircase landed in the center of the house, and all directions led somewhere else. The mudroom and back door were at the end of a short hallway, directly behind where she stood. Another offshoot led to—she peeked through a swinging door—the kitchen. She normally wasn't so nosy, but Gideon hadn't told her she couldn't look around.

She raised on the balls of her bare feet for long seconds before she committed herself. Then started off.

The kitchen was a mess. Someone had make breakfast, but the remains of eggs stuck in a pan on the stovetop, now brown. A biscuit pan was empty of bread, but had rings of cooked-on residue where it hadn't been scraped. A pile of plates sat next to the sink.

The countertops were littered with old mail, other assorted dishes and a...she didn't know what kind of farm implement it was, but the pronged tool looked dangerous. And like it belonged in the barn, not the kitchen. The cabinets were dated, the stain almost worn off in some places. The wallpaper was faded, and the fridge an old model.

The entire room was in need of an update and a thorough cleaning. Matt had said Gideon ran the ranch with several "hands"—cowboys, she thought. Did the mess really not bother the group of bachelors?

She wandered through the room and into a dining room. Only it was like no dining room she'd seen before. A rough-hewn wooden picnic table took up the center of the room. It would've been country charming if there had been any decoration to go with it. The table was bare, walls were bare, even the hardwood floor could've used a rug. And a good scrubbing.

Well, it was...functional. Certainly big enough to seat ten or so men. Maybe eight, if they were all as large as Gideon.

She edged past the table and back through the entryway she'd passed through earlier. This time, she kept going instead of turning back to the center staircase.

The family room had a lived-in look. The two low couches bookended a coffee table that had so many water rings that it almost seemed planned. A flat-screen TV took up one wall, and opposite that, a large rock fireplace appeared inviting. But there was no throw over the back of the couch, no homey touches anywhere.

She wandered through the entryway and past the staircase to the back corner of the house, the only place she hadn't explored. There were three doorways off the hall here. Bathroom. Linen closet. Bedroom.

She stood in the doorway, frozen for a long moment. The bed was made, a simple quilt thrown across it as bedspread. Curtains framed the window looking out on blue sky. A dresser was cluttered with a collection of spare change and, in the back corner, a huge, gold belt buckle.

On the side table stood two pictures. One was Matt, a woman that must be his sister, and... could that clean-shaven man be Gideon?

He was handsome. With his chiseled jaw and those sharp eyes, laugh lines fanning from his eyes... he would have caught her eye if they'd met in different circumstances.

Was this Gideon's room?

In the picture, a gray-haired man stood behind the three, his arms stretched to encompass them. Their father?

Behind the picture was another. She'd stepped into the room before she really meant to. Close enough to see the photo.

It was a candid shot of several men in camouflage sitting around in the desert. They were heavily armed with scary-looking black guns in hand. In this one, Gideon sported a shorter, trimmed beard and dark sunglasses.

He was laughing.

Something tugged deep in the pit of her stomach. A response to the man, even though he wasn't here.

She shouldn't be in his room. She backed up even as she realized she'd intruded into his personal domain.

She wouldn't like it if he'd invaded the inner sanctuary of her rooms back at the palace. He'd probably hate knowing she was in here.

She quickly ducked out of the room and regrouped in the hallway, wrapping her arms around her middle.

What had happened to that smiling soldier? What had turned him into a surly grizzly bear?

Her thoughts dissipated.

Even though she stood in a patch of sunlight slanting in from the large picture windows in the living room, she didn't feel warm.

She was here, on a ranch in the middle of nowhere, Texas. She was safe.

But there was a part of her, a big part, that was also lost.

LACY WILLIAMS

CHAPTER FOUR

If Alessandra had expected Gideon to be the worst-groomed of the cowhands, she would've been sorely disappointed that evening.

After the past, crazy forty-odd hours, she'd hit a wall sometime in the early afternoon. She'd dragged herself upstairs to lie down on the bed and only wakened when the noise level in the house below rose loud enough that it shook the rafters.

She was still mulling over Gideon's hesitant invitation. Should she go downstairs and join the party?

There was a small mirror on the tall chest of drawers next to the twin bed in the room she'd been given, and she squinted at her reflection in the fading light filtering through the curtains. Squinted her eyes more tightly together, so she wouldn't have to see the rat's nest that was her hair. The braid she'd put in earlier had come halfway apart, and one side of her hair stuck up in a matted mess where she'd slept on

li

222222

it.

This was one time she wouldn't have minded having her stylist on hand. She'd never had to worry about getting her hair right, because Anna was there to help her.

She untangled the rest of the braid and picked up the brush that Gideon had found for her somewhere. It pulled her hair when she began the first strokes. She'd showered earlier, and the conditioner was a cheap brand that made her hair feel rough between her fingers.

She didn't even have her own toiletries.

She stifled the whine that wanted to escape and set about brushing her hair and then pulling it into a tight French braid that hopefully wouldn't look as messy as she felt inside.

A quick stop in the bathroom to splash her face and pinch her cheeks—neither did she have any makeup—and she forced herself to the head of the stairs.

Her stomach rumbled, making the decision for her.

Plus, there was no use hiding up here. She had a hunch Matt would come looking for her, even if the irascible Gideon wouldn't.

Downstairs, it was even louder. Men's voices and raucous laughter rang out through the house. The swinging door to the kitchen was closed, but she could hear the clanging of dishes and the movement of what might have been two people in there.

Most of the noise was coming from the living room.

She hesitated in the shadowed hall, looking in.

Gideon was closest to her, on the other side of the large open archway. He stood with feet slightly apart and arms crossed, what might be a scowl under his beard.

On the far couch, two men she didn't recognize lounged negligently, their dusty boots stretched out in front of them. She winced, thinking about the floor. One still wore a cowboy hat and let his head loll back on the couch. Both of them looked as if they'd been in their faded, dirty clothes for days. And both sported long, unkempt beards, like Gideon wore. Was this a Texas thing? Or a ranch hand thing? Did no one wash up for supper?

Matt perched on a barstool across the room, talking animatedly with another man, this one with a shock of short-cropped red hair. She couldn't see his face.

She must've moved, or maybe Gideon just sensed her presence, because his head turned toward her before she was ready to be spotted.

He cleared his throat and the room quieted

instantly, everyone's attention on him.

"Guys, this is the little gal I was telling you about. Meet Allie."

She stepped into the light as three pairs of eyes—plus Matt's glinting gaze—swiveled toward her.

She'd keynoted enough that she was used to being the center of attention. Used to being in the spotlight, having cameras pointed at her. But this...she felt their attention acutely.

"Nate and Trey there on the couch," Gideon said with a nod.

She tried to smile, but it felt tremulous.

"And Brian," he motioned to the redhead near Matt. "Chase and Dan are putting the finishing touches on supper."

Often at public events, she had an aide nearby at all times to whisper a name in her ear or prompt her into conversation before she could make a mistake.

She floundered now.

"Thank you for opening your home to me," she said softly.

"It's Gideon's place," either Trey or Nate said from the couch with a big grin. "Interesting that he brought you out here. He usually keeps his distance from any pretty woman."

Trey-slash-Nate cut him off with an elbow to the ribs, eliciting a huff of air from the other man.

Gideon growled.

"It's my place too," Matt said easily, diverting attention from his brother.

"For now." Gideon said. "Not sure how long me'n Carrie will let you keep your shares, since you're pretty much career military."

She let her gaze slide to Gideon. Had he helped Matt avert the conversation from her purposely?

"He's never liked shoveling—" Brian started to say something crude but caught himself halfway through the word with a glance at Alessandra. Splotches of red climbed in his cheeks—he was clean shaven. "Sorry, ma'am."

She let it go with a shrug and a smile. She had no intention of coming in here and asking these men to change their lifestyles to suit her. They were doing *her* a favor.

But a glance at Gideon showed his face looked like a thundercloud.

Then someone knocked on the door. Matt jumped up from his stool.

She moved out of the way as Matt came toward her, heading for the door. He didn't quite get it open.

"Uncle Matt!"

The exuberant cry preceded a tornado of a small brunette girl who launched herself through the doorway at her uncle. Matt swept her up easily into his arms. A woman who must be Carrie, Gideon and Matt's sister, stepped over the threshold, and she too threw herself at Matt. He caught her too.

Alessandra caught the small sob that escaped the woman, even though her face was buried in Matt's shoulder.

Alessandra was intruding.

Her gaze connected with Gideon's where he stood opposite, behind the cluster of his family.

If she wasn't mistaken, his eyes had a sheen of moisture too.

~ * ~

Gideon was intensely aware of Alessandra at the dinner table, two seats away with his niece Scarlett between them.

Part of him really wanted to know what the princess thought of their gathering. This must be a lot different than what she was used to. The hands were in fine form, boisterous and loud as they showed off for both women. The one-course meal of hearty spaghetti and meatballs, salad and crusty garlic bread, was probably much simpler fare than she was used to. Their cutlery could never be called *silver*ware. And Apollo made a practice of crawling on the floor beneath the table, licking up any crumb that dared be dropped.

Although Scarlett had clung to Matt for a good ten minutes when his sister had arrived, she'd elected to sit next to Gideon at the supper table, and somehow wrangled Alessandra into the chair on her other side. With the shortie between them, he kept catching glances, finding himself in the laser sight of Alessandra's bright smile.

Although she was definitely out of place—quiet and unassuming—he caught the tail end of several of her smiles in response to something the guys or Scarlett had said. She was fresh, like a spring tulip. The diamond in a room full of coal lumps.

Once, when she'd laughed at something dumb Nate had said, Gideon had gotten a bite of meatball lodged in his esophagus. It stayed there, a hard lump that had him shifting uncomfortably in his seat.

He felt old. Out of place. Grumpy. Just like Matt had said earlier.

His brother was quieter than usual. Gideon still believed something had happened during his tour. Gideon had had one or two near-fatal incidents, and when you came home after something like that...well, it changed how you looked at things. How you treated the people you cared about.

He just wished his little brother hadn't had to go through it.

"Uncle Gid," Scarlett piped, distracting him from his thoughts.

"Yeah, squirt?" He never got tired of looking at the little upturned face.

Scarlett was four going on twenty-five, and he was a sucker for the freckles splashed across the bridge of her pert nose and those big, cornflower blue eyes.

Scarlett scooted close, her little shoulder brushing his elbow. She motioned for him to lean down. So he did, aware of Alessandra's attention on the two of them.

"I think Allie is a princess." Scarlett's breath was warm and smelled of garlic, and it distracted him long enough that he had to play her words over a second time before he grasped their meaning.

His stomach somersaulted. If his four-year-old niece could recognize Alessandra, they were in for a world of trouble. Had Carrie been playing the national news channel at home?

"What makes you think that, squirt?" Somehow he managed to get the words out evenly.

"Look how long her hair is," the pipsqueak whispered, her head bumping his chin as she turned to shoot a look at their guest and then quickly turned back when Alessandra caught her looking. "I think she's Rapunzel."

Reality intruded as his eyes focused on the long

braid that hung down Alessandra's back and past her waist. Rapunzel, indeed.

"I don't know, squirt," he said softly. "She looks kinda regular to me."

Not really. Even wearing clothes that were similar to every one else's at the table, there was a different air to Alessandra. It wasn't entirely her posture—although she sat straighter than anyone he'd ever met, as if she balanced a book on her head at all times—and she hadn't tilted her nose up once. It was something else. Just *her*, maybe. She was too fine.

Whatever it was, she didn't belong here.

Tired of waiting on him or maybe dissatisfied with his answer, Scarlett turned to the princess. "Are you Rapunzel?"

"No, I'm not," Alessandra answered. "Is she your favorite princess?"

Scarlett shrugged. "I like the ice princess and her sister."

He didn't figure she was up on the latest animated princess movies, but Alessandra leaned closer to Scarlett. "Oh, I like her too. But really, the reindeer is my favorite character from that movie. Do you know the song he sings?"

She hummed a few bars until Scarlett belted out some words that sounded like gibberish to him, then both females dissolved into giggles.

Someone kicked his foot from beneath the table. He glared across to see his sister, squished in between Matt and Brian, watching him speculatively.

His ranch hands weren't as subtle.

"Boss, you planning on needing some time off?" Dan asked from the other end of the table. "Maybe doing some courting?"

Guffaws went around the room.

Fire flared in his cheeks, but hopefully the beard camouflaged it. Scarlett was chattering to the princess, so maybe they'd missed the joke at his expense.

He wasn't sitting here mooning over the girl. He was listening in to make sure she didn't slip up and put his family in danger. Protecting Scarlett.

That was it.

If he did feel a bolt of attraction, he would never have an opportunity to act on it. Right. Imagine someone like *her* taking up with him. They'd rub each other the wrong way. What about him attending a palace function? They'd probably want to sprinkle glitter in his beard.

But an uncomfortable clutch of his chest remained.

~ * ~

The group sat around the table, talking, for a long time after supper. Scarlett relocated to Matt's knee, regaling her uncle of tales about her preschool friends while Matt listened attentively. Gideon would have to get to the bottom of what was bugging his brother eventually.

Scarlett's desertion left a space between him and the princess, and he noticed Alessandra disappear from the table before too long. She'd probably gone upstairs to sleep. Or relax. Or whatever. Was probably bored with their simple talk of ranching and the folks in town. It was for the best, anyway. She'd be here a few days, maybe, then go back to her ritzy life.

The hands had accepted his explanation of a damsel in trouble without asking for a lot of details— but apparently they wanted to believe she was more to him than a mere acquaintance.

Ha.

When he carried his plate from the table into the kitchen, he found her elbow-deep in a sink full of sudsy water, scrubbing pots. Apollo lay at her feet, his black nose resting on brown paws.

Seeing her like this made that uncomfortable pinch in his chest return full bore.

Of all the things he'd imagined her doing, the dishes wasn't one of them. Had the noise of their conversations completed drowned out the clanking of pots and pans, the swish of the water?

"Everything okay?" he asked.

She startled and looked over her shoulder at him, their gazes connecting again. He easily read the shadows in her eyes.

"I'm fine." The firm set of her lips might indicate otherwise.

He wasn't going to push her, not now.

"We're kind of a rowdy bunch," he said. Not really apologizing. And stating the obvious.

She *hmmed*, but didn't agree or disagree.

"Sort of an acquired taste. Like black coffee. Or sushi."

This time, he won a small smile, seen only because she'd turned her head slightly toward him. He didn't know why it mattered, but seeing it made the tight knot in his chest loosen up, just slightly.

"Don't blame you at all for needing to take us in small doses."

She smiled again, just a small twitch of her mouth, but shook her head. Agreeing that his hands and his family were best a teaspoon at time? Or was she disagreeing?

She didn't explain.

"Nobody expects you to clean up after us, you know." He deposited his dirty plate and fork on the counter near her. It was conspicuously clean, as if it'd been freshly scrubbed—and the counter along the opposite side of the sink was laid out with clean dishes drying on towels. She'd been busy.

He moved to her other side. He picked up the last towel on the line she'd laid out and started drying the nearest item, the scrambled eggs skillet from this morning. It was spotless. He well knew how the egg residue cemented to the pan when it was left all day. And that was only one of the dishes that had littered the kitchen.

It even smelled cleaner in here. Like lemons.

He might've thought that Brian—on dinner duty—had cleaned up, if he didn't know his men so well. They preferred to leave the mess until there were no more dishes to use before anyone would take initiative.

"Inspecting my work?" she asked. Her attention remained on the pot she was vigorously scrubbing. He winced. Was it from yesterday? Or two days ago?

"No..."

But she must've heard the weak denial in his tone, because she frowned as she scrubbed even harder. "Maybe you think a pr—" She glanced over her shoulder. So did he. They were alone. "A person like me wouldn't know how to wash dishes."

That was exactly what he'd thought. Didn't being

born a princess mean she'd grown up with a silver spoon in her mouth?

~ * ~

It shouldn't bother Alessandra that Gideon thought she was unable to perform a simple task, such as doing dishes. It wasn't exactly a skill she was known for.

She used the dishrag to scrub at one particular caked-on bit of gunk in the bottom corner of the pan. "When I was fourteen..." Soon after her father had started to seriously decline. "I started sneaking down to the kitchens in the wee hours of the morning. Our on-staff chef put me to work. Baking bread, helping with breakfast...and other things. He believed that anyone working in his kitchen should know how to clean up after themselves. Even me."

Chef Marco had become like a beloved uncle to her, though he was paid staff. Even as a teen, she'd known better than to air the family's private business to anyone. So even though she'd never talked about the overwhelming grief of watching her father decline, Marco had known. Had provided a steady presence, even as he put on a gruff outward act of not wanting the princess in his domain.

Marco and Krissy and Bella, two of the

housemaids, had been more of a family to her than anyone else, but as her responsibilities to represent Glorvaird grew, she'd grown more distant from them.

Thinking about her sort-of-staff, sort-of-friends was why she'd eventually had to leave the group of boisterous cowboys and Carrie and Scarlett. She missed the familiar. Missed home.

More than anything, she'd wanted a family like this one. Oh, they didn't all have DNA ties, but it was clear that the cowhands had an affection for each other, even through the ribbing and teasing. It was also clear they respected Gideon and his leadership as he ran the place.

Her own family...well, her father and older sister were difficult. And Mia, her younger sister, was often gone, flitting around social events.

He hadn't responded to her story about helping in the kitchen, and she glanced at him to see his brow furrowed above the flat cookie tray he was drying.

She nudged his elbow with hers and tried for a smile. "It isn't as if I haven't made judgments about you, too."

She couldn't pinpoint what exactly made her spout the teasing statement. There was safety in being reserved, holding herself separate from someone she would likely only know for a matter of days. But something inside her wanted to erase the deep grooves in his forehead.

"What do you mean?"

"Just that." She was unable to prevent her lips from twitching with a smile at his frown.

She motioned to his face. "I spent the entire morning thinking of you as *Gideon the Bear*, because of how you go around growling and grunting at everyone. And, well...you seem sort of dangerous..." She trailed off. She'd meant to say something about his dark, overgrown beard and hair that needed a trim, even motioned in a halfhearted circle toward his head. She'd meant to make him smile. It hadn't worked.

His frown didn't lift. It deepened. Her stomach pitched.

"But," she continued quickly, "when you're with your niece, you're more of a teddy bear." She'd been shocked at first, to see him smiling with Scarlett, who obviously had him wrapped around her little finger.

She'd even heard him chuckle once. Seen the flash of white teeth behind his beard. His eyes had *sparkled*.

Those moments had been like looking at a totally different man. An attractive one, like the picture she'd stumbled upon in his bedroom.

"So my initial assessment was wrong," she said quickly, before her thoughts could get—more—out of control. "Or at least, not completely correct. You have a tough side that was probably necessary as an active-duty soldier. And you also have a...sweet side."

She snapped her mouth shut, realizing she was babbling. And blundering. She'd nearly scrubbed the finish off the pot and quickly moved to rinse it in the second sink.

There was no avoiding Gideon as she upended the damp pot on one of the drying towels. He set aside the towel and leaned one hip against the countertop. Crossed his arms over his chest.

Her face burned. She certainly hadn't meant to say so much. There was something about him that made her nervous.

She barely dared to look up into his eyes, afraid she'd offended him in some way. When she did, she couldn't read his expression. His eyes glittered slightly, but the masked emotion could be anger or humor or anything, really.

Finally, he spoke. "So you're saying you're a"—his eyes widened slightly—"*you-know-what*, who likes to do dishes."

His nostrils flared slightly, and one corner of his mouth tipped up. He was teasing her?

Movement from behind them broke the moment, and she flushed, quickly going back to the sink, though the mountain of dirty dishes had been reduced to a more manageable hill.

"Gideon, are you picking on your houseguest?" It was Carrie's strident voice. "You don't have to clean up after these pigs—I mean bachelors—honey."

The other woman touched Alessandra's shoulder, a gesture meant to convey solidarity, but the unexpected touch startled her. People usually weren't so familiar. Of course, Carrie didn't know her true identity either, or she might not get so close.

Alessandra hated the subterfuge, though she understood why it was necessary.

Gideon backed away, raising both hands in front of himself. "I didn't make her do anything. I walked in, and she was already halfway through the pile."

Carrie moved into the place beside Alessandra that he'd recently vacated, picking up the damp towel and twisting it into some kind of snapping weapon that she wielded to drive him out of the room. She joined Alessandra beside the sink and took up the task of drying, much more efficiently than Gideon had.

"I don't know what kind of trouble you're in," Carrie said, voice low, "and I don't need to know. Gideon and his boys will take care of you."

Alessandra didn't know whether the woman was gearing up for a warning, but she braced herself anyway.

"I just wanted you to know that if you need a

woman to talk to, I'm not too far away. My place in town is only about a ten-minute drive from here. I work afternoons, while Scarlett is in school."

The offer was so unexpected that tears welled in Alessandra's eyes. She blinked them back. "Thank you."

"I'm planning on making a run out here in the morning, after I drop Scarlett at class. I doubt either of my brothers thought to provide you anything more than a bar of rough soap and a change of clothes. I've got some things you can borrow, and I'll stop by the drug store for the essentials."

Carrie's words were so true that Alessandra couldn't help the wet giggle that emerged. "Thank you. Very much."

Carrie shook her head in an exaggerated manner. "We grew up together, but I don't think I rubbed off on them all that much. They don't know an eyelash curler from a flat iron, and heaven forbid you start crying in front of them. Easiest way to get rid of them in a pinch, by the way. Of course, Mom was gone by the time we were teenagers."

Alessandra handed Carrie the next dish. They were down to the supper plates now, the water in the sink grown tepid. "My mother died when I was five."

They shared a glance. It was a unifying thing. Losing a mother was something you never quite got over.

They finished the rest of the dishes in no time at all, Gideon's sister carrying the conversation, mostly talking about Scarlett. There was no mention of Scarlett's father, and Alessandra couldn't help wondering what had happened to him, though she didn't get up the guts to ask.

They wiped off their hands on clean towels. Alessandra's were pruny from being in the water so long. Carrie kept her eyes down. "About Gideon... He's got a good heart, but...he won't open up. Don't expect too much from him."

Carrie raised her head, her eyes trying to impart the message that Alessandra was struggling to comprehend. "I-I won't," she said, because that's what Carrie seemed to expect.

Did everyone thing she and Gideon were involved? She remembered his earlier statement at the diner that he hadn't dated in a long while. Were his friends and family just seeing what they wanted to see?

Was there any use in telling the other woman that she had absolutely no expectations of Gideon? He'd offered her sanctuary while the royal security force worked with the Glorvaird and New York law enforcement teams to investigate the shooting and bombing. When the head of palace security was able to find her a secure way home, she'd return to the family duty that awaited her.

Carrie surprised her with a goodbye hug. Alessandra had to fight not to tighten up at the familiarity.

It made her nose sting.

When was the last time one of her own sisters had hugged her?

She couldn't remember.

LACY WILLIAMS

CHAPTER FIVE

That same night, Gideon stayed late in the birthing barn. He watched a mama giving birth, just making sure everything went the way it was supposed to.

He was afraid to go back to the house. Afraid that, even though it was late, he would run into Alessandra again. That she'd start rambling in that adorable way that made him want to smile. Or hug her.

Gideon the Bear.

There was a little jagged piece of broken mirror nailed to one of the studs on the far wall, and he caught a bit of his scowling reflection.

The Bear.

It wasn't the worst thing he'd been called in his life.

He tilted his head slightly, catching sight of the unkempt hair and scraggly beard. He looked like a mountain man. A little like a real bear.

He jerked his chin up, and there was that scowl again in the reflection.

He didn't really growl and grunt all the time, did he? He ran his hand through his beard, a little ashamed of himself. Since when did he not care?

Sure, he had high expectations. He paid his hands better than any other ranch around, and if they slacked off on the job, it ticked him off. The Triple H ran a large herd and every cog had to operate.

And when someone hitched an unexpected ride in his truck, something that could potentially put his family in danger, he might've come off a little grumpy...

Was that really how she saw him? How everybody saw him? She'd seemed to admire his interaction with Scarlett, but the rest hadn't been very complimentary.

And she'd been right. He'd judged her harshly, thinking she didn't have any experience with domestic chores.

He didn't know what to think about her story about hanging out in the kitchens with the royal chef. There had been a slight pause when she'd begun the story. One that made him think there was more behind the story than she'd told him.

Or was that just his suspicious, grizzly-like nature, rearing its head?

There was a computer in the tack room, in the area of the barn closed off to protect it from the elements. It was an old one, but it had Internet access.

He took one last look at the cow and decided she could work on her own for awhile before he pushed through the door toward the tack room.

It took longer than he would've liked for the old machine to boot up, but within a few minutes he was logged on to the Internet, searching for everything he could find about her family. Something he probably should've done earlier in the day, and would've if he hadn't lost time bringing the princess out here and then checking in with all the hands.

Her mom had passed away when she was little. He felt a sympathetic pang, because it was something they had in common. There were some old mentions of concerns over the King's health, but they seemed to taper off after a few years.

The crown princess, Alessandra's older sister, had been in a car accident as a preteen and bore scars across her face and torso. She had been basically out of public sight, no pictures or anything, until her coronation when she came of age at eighteen. He'd seen worse. She would never be a grand beauty, but he didn't think the scars detracted that much from her looks. The gossip rags, however, claimed she had a beastly personality. He couldn't find one picture of her smiling, and sure enough, in several paparazzi shots, she wore a nasty snarl across her face.

Alessandra's younger sister seemed to be in the media all the time. Her bubbly smile came through in pixels, and he could guess she enjoyed the attention. She was young but seemed to be on the arm of several handsome young men at different times. A social butterfly? Or did she enjoy toying with young men's affections? It was impossible to know.

Alessandra didn't get as much media coverage as either of her sisters. She appeared regularly at charity events and palace-sponsored occasions. Her smile was much more reserved than her younger sister's. After interacting with her today, he didn't think what he was studying on his screen was her real smile at all.

At breakfast, she'd claimed her aunt might be behind the bombing and assassination attempt. He searched for information on a possible family feud but didn't find much. The king's sister had been estranged since her eighteenth birthday. She'd married and had two sons, now about the same age as Alessandra and her sisters. The reason for the estrangement wasn't publicized. Nothing was mentioned anywhere about the aunt's relationship to the crown being revoked. Which meant the king's nephews were technically princes in their own right.

What could make a woman hate the king and his daughters so much that she tried to kill them?

It wasn't his job to find out. It wasn't even really his job to protect Alessandra, but he'd taken it on. He'd give Cash a couple of days for reconnaissance, and hopefully things would settle down enough for her to go home.

He couldn't wait for things to get back to normal.

~ * ~

Alessandra couldn't sleep.

She'd gone to bed, even dozed a little, but nightmares quickly followed. Of those awful moments when Tim had surged toward her in the crowd. The muted *pop!* of the gun discharging. And Tim's blood after he'd knocked her to the ground.

Then the scene went a little fuzzy.

Her dream-self pressed harder on Tim's chest, trying to save him. Only something had changed. She looked closely at his face and realized her dream self was pressing on *Gideon's* chest. That it was *Gideon's* broken body beneath her hands.

She woke with a gasp.

She bolted up in the twin bed, breathed deeply.

The bed was safe. Lumpier than anything she was used to, but safe. She tucked the quilt over her knees and wrapped her arms around herself.

She couldn't deal with whatever part of her

subconscious had put Gideon into the dream. Surely it was because he'd been kind to her, and he'd been one of the last people she'd seen before she'd gone to bed. And he was protecting her.

That was all there was to it, right?

She grieved for Tim, tears falling now as she thought about the man who'd given his life for her. Who would comfort his sister and mother back in Glorvaird?

Until now, she hadn't paid attention to the other thoughts that she'd shoved away after Tim's death. But questions swirled now. How had a killer gotten so close to her? Close enough that her bodyguard had barely had time to step into the line of fire? Although some events she attended were publicized on the palace website and in the media, her exact schedule was never confirmed. Tim had been her only bodyguard, but there was a team of hired men and women who scouted each location, each function she attended beforehand. And everyone in that crowd was supposed to have been invited to the party.

She didn't have answers.

She also didn't think her aunt—if that's who'd initiated the bombing and the shooting—would give up. She didn't know the woman personally, and Father didn't talk about her much, but there were always whispers among the staff about her aunt's unhappiness with the way her father ruled the country. Helena wanted to rule.

But because of the bloodlines, she would have to kill all of them—the king and his three daughters—before she would be crowned. Would the people of Glorvaird even accept her if she was behind the killings? Perhaps that's why it was so hard to connect the attempted killings to anyone. Her aunt was covering her tracks, and well.

Or perhaps it hadn't been her aunt after all, though Alessandra couldn't think of another party with such violent intentions toward her family. Glorvaird was a small, peaceful country that relied on trade with its neighbors and worked to keep peaceful agreements in place.

Knowing her swirling thoughts weren't conducive to sleep, Alessandra got out of bed. The bedroom was bare and simple, with not even a television to distract her.

Because she had only the clothes that Gideon had given her, she'd gone to bed in just a T-shirt and undergarments. Now she pulled the jeans back on. Then she slipped into the hallway.

She paused on the top step, one hand covering the smile that bloomed. She hadn't heard it from inside her room, but heavy snores emanated from most of the upstairs bedrooms. She knew the ranch hands worked hard. Guessed they played hard. Apparently, they slept hard, too.

She crept downstairs, but there was no sign of anyone else awake. The microwave clock in the kitchen read one a.m. and she guessed the crew had to be out working early.

But knowing that didn't get her any closer to a restful state. She needed something to *do*.

And she found it in the kitchen.

She'd finished the dishes earlier, but Carrie had shooed her out before she'd attacked any of the other cleaning issues. Not that she hadn't noticed and catalogued them.

The countertops and window needed a good washing. As did the microwave, stovetop, and oven. Even the shelves in the cabinets wore a layer of dust between where the dishes rested.

And the floor was desperately in need of a good mopping.

She turned on the soft light over the sink, not the full overhead light, hoping that she wouldn't wake Gideon in his back bedroom. She found a plethora of cleaning supplies beneath the sink. Mostly unopened.

And she set to work.

~ * ~

Gideon had slept hard after foolishly being out in the barn so late—for the second night in a row. He woke abruptly.

Something was wrong.

Light streamed through his window, which meant he'd overslept by at least an hour and a half. The clock read seven-thirty.

The hands were going to give him heck for sleeping in.

He emerged from his room minutes later, running one hand through his hair. And stopped cold.

Someone had baked. The sweet smell of cinnamon and sugar wafted through the house.

He found Dan and Trey standing in the foyer, a plate in each of their hands, shoveling food into their mouths. Judging from the crumbs on their plates, they'd enjoyed...were those cinnamon rolls? And some kind of pie made from eggs and vegetables. They were staring into the living room until he approached, and then Dan started to swivel away, defending the remaining eggs on his plate.

"What's going on?" Gideon asked.

"Shh," Trey shushed him with a scandalized look into the living room.

Gideon frowned and stepped forward so he could

see.

Alessandra was curled up on the far couch. Sleeping. One hand was tucked beneath her face. Her hair was loose and wavy—probably from the braid she'd worn yesterday—and formed a cloud all around her.

Why wasn't she upstairs, in her own bed?

"She must've made breakfast," Dan murmured from behind him. "Sticky buns and quiche in the oven when I got up."

"Cleaned the whole kitchen too," Trey whispered.

Gideon hadn't been able to tear his gaze from the sleeping princess, but now he registered the spray bottle and dirty rag on the low table not far from where she lay.

He sniffed again, this time registering the scent of lemony soap beneath the food smells. *She'd cleaned?*

Sure enough, his boots didn't stick to the kitchen floor when he finally turned them that direction. The appliances were *shiny*. Even the sunlight seemed to sparkle through the window. Everything was spotless.

"Cleaning fairy got us in here, too," Matt called out from the dining room.

Gideon bypassed the tray of buns and the dish with eggs that sat on the stovetop—for now—to stick his head through the doorway. Matt, Nate,

Brian and Chase all lounged around the table, stuffing their faces. The dog was under the table again.

"Why are you all not at work already?"

"Breakfast," Brian slurred, his mouth full. A piece of eggs zoomed out of his overly full mouth and landed on the table.

Gideon winced. "Do you think someone who spent the night cleaning up after you lot wants to do it all over again? Have a little respect."

Brian looked appropriately abashed and used his fingers to scoop the egg back onto his plate.

"You're gonna keep her around, aren't you?" Chase asked hopefully.

"Yeah," Nate chimed in. "She's a mighty good cook."

Brian swallowed the rest of his food. "Not sure what she sees in you, but you've got to turn on some kind of charm and keep her around."

"Yeah," chimed Trey, as he and Dan joined the crowd from the doorway off the front hall.

Matt's eyes glittered as he looked to Gideon, waiting for the answer like everyone else. Matt should know better than to wear that expression. The woman was a *princess*.

There was no way she could stay, but Gideon couldn't tell the boys that.

He sighed. "I told you yesterday, she's in trouble. Just needs a place to lay low for a few days." But he couldn't resist teasing them. "Besides, do you really think someone like her"—he jerked his finger over his shoulder—"would want to hang around a bunch of hands who think personal grooming is optional and don't even know how to clean up after themselves?"

Matt grinned, shoving another forkful of food into his mouth. The other hands looked down at themselves. They were a rough bunch. Other than Carrie, they didn't interact much with women. Didn't spend much time in town. There wasn't much need to trim a beard or get a haircut. Or buy new clothes.

Like he was one to talk, anyway. She'd called him *Gideon the Bear.* Not just for his personality.

It wasn't as if it mattered anyway, because she'd be leaving soon. They'd go back to their regular routines, and she'd go back to her palace. She wouldn't be around to appreciate it if they all up and decided to shave and wear clean clothes anyway.

But the thought remained lodged in his gut, a boulder.

Matt stood and headed toward the kitchen. Gideon followed, leaving the other hands muttering around the kitchen table.

"Thought I'd saddle up Rufus and do some fence

line checking," Matt said as he moved to wash his plate and cup in the sink. Gideon was glad to see that his brother, at least, wouldn't leave more of a mess for Alessandra. "It's been awhile since I've had a good ride."

Gideon nodded slowly, mentally running over the list of things he'd planned to do today. He made a snap decision. "I'll ride with you. We can catch up. Scarlett and Carrie weren't the only ones who missed you, you know."

It would give him a chance to talk to Matt, see if he could figure out what was causing the shadows in his brother's eyes.

Two hours later, Gideon was enjoying the familiar feel of the horse beneath him and the sounds of the horses whickering to each other.

Even though sometimes he ached to be back with the Teams, this land was part of him.

But a chill wind blew through his coat, and he hadn't gotten any closer to answers about what was going on with Matt. He'd asked about his brother's tour and gotten deflected. Asked if Matt had any romantic prospects, wondering if maybe his brother was having woman problems, and gotten shut down. There was maybe something there, but his brother wasn't talking.

They had been close in high school, before

Gideon had left for the Navy. But that didn't necessarily mean they'd shared each other's confidences. Gideon had stood up for Matt once in a fistfight. Matt had covered for him when a prank had gone wrong.

But they didn't talk about their feelings. They were guys. They just didn't.

Which made it hard now to figure out how to help.

Gideon was left with a nagging feeling that something had happened on tour. But if Matt didn't want to talk about it, how could he get it out of him?

He was on the verge of giving up when he spotted a flash of white against a dark patch of mud, several yards away. He wheeled his horse closer.

Was that a cigarette butt? None of the hands smoked.

He hopped off the horse, bending to examine it. Picked it up. It *was* a butt.

He showed it to Matt, who didn't seem upset about it. "Could've been from someone who snuck on the place to visit the fishing pond."

"Or from someone scouting the place." Gideon didn't like the feel of it. Out of place. On the heels of the princess's arrival.

"Listen, Nate came to me last night, while you were in the barn."

Gideon looked up, still not convinced about the butt, but he flicked it back on the ground.

"He said you're treating him like a hand, not the foreman. You trying to edge him out of his job?"

"*What?*" *Bear.* How long would Alessandra's nickname haunt him?

"You've got to give a man room to do his job," Matt said.

"He's got plenty of room to do it, long as he and the hands get it right."

"You sure that's how he feels?"

Gideon didn't know. He did know he was frustrated at not knowing whether the cigarette butt was something to be worried about. Now this.

He wasn't a micro-manager, not really. Was that how the hands saw him?

He didn't know how much mental energy he could give to this, with a princess to watch out for. It was just one more thing for him to add to his never-ending list.

CHAPTER SIX

Around lunchtime, Gideon got a call from Cash that there was some chatter about continuing plots against the Glorvaird royalty.

Which was exactly what he didn't want to hear.

According to Cash, there were no whispers of the princess's location, but after finding the cigarette butt that shouldn't have been there, he spent the afternoon scouting for any other signs that a stranger had been on the ranch.

Hours of riding and tracking didn't turn up anything else, but he couldn't get rid of the sense that someone with an agenda had been here. He'd learned to trust his gut, and his gut was hardly ever wrong.

He spent the next hour in the barn, making calls to locals, asking if they'd seen any suspicious activity. Probably they all thought he was nuts, but he couldn't help that.

The sun was setting and his stomach was growling when he headed across the yard for the house. He hated the feeling of blindness. Hated thinking someone could be watching the place, and he wouldn't know until it was too late.

As he crossed the yard, the back door opened, and the princess appeared, stepping out onto the back porch. Out in the open.

The hair on the back of his neck rose all at once, and he took the porch steps at a run. "Get back," he ordered, but either she didn't share his sense of urgency or she didn't realize anything was wrong, because instead of moving, she froze.

Which meant that he collided with her, full body, knocking her off her feet. He heard her gasp as he swept her along with him, quickly thumping her back against the clapboard siding. It wasn't enough to keep her out of sight, so he tucked her head into his shoulder, too.

"I told you to stay inside," he said harshly, breath sawing in and out of his chest. Adrenaline pulsed through his veins with every throb of his heart.

She said something, but it was muffled against his chest, and he couldn't make it out.

He shuffled the both of them two feet to the left and yanked open the screen door before he pushed her inside, careful to keep himself between her and any possible threat.

Only when he had slammed the interior door shut

and bodily pushed her several feet into the mudroom did he take a deep breath.

"What's the matter? Gideon?" That was Carrie's voice, coming from the kitchen.

Alessandra watched him with eyes wide and dark with fear. All the color had leached from her face.

"Gideon, let go of her."

He still held both of the princess's shoulders, though now she was at arms' length and not pressed close to him. Her flowery scent was burned into his nostrils, into his brain.

"Gideon," Carrie said again.

He shook himself out of the moment, dropped his hands to his sides, realizing for the first time with some clarity that Alessandra was dressed up. Oh, not dressed up, per se, but differently than she had been yesterday. She wore some kind of fuzzy sweater over a pale yellow dress that flared around her knees. It made her look feminine and soft, and with her hair down and wavy...

He didn't know what to do with the attraction that welled almost violently inside him, riding the tide of his rioting adrenaline and blood pressure.

He backed up a step and used one hand to take off his hat; the other he swept through his hair, hoping the motion might hide any hint of the turmoil he was experiencing.

"What were you doing outside?" he barked.

"I was coming to look for you. Matt said he thought you were still in the barn. It's suppertime."

Suppertime. When was the last time someone had cared enough to make sure he came in for supper? Something twisted in his stomach.

But the fear he'd felt when he'd seen her out in the open remained.

His nostrils flared as he contemplated what he might do to his brother. "He should've told you to stay inside. Why didn't you just call my cell?"

Carrie was still approaching, waving a wooden spoon in his direction. "I was watching through the window and saw you barrel into Allie. Her head hit the wall pretty hard—I heard the *clunk* from inside."

Had he done that?

"Can you give us a minute?" he asked his sister, and if the words weren't completely polite, Carrie must've seen in his expression that he was shaken up, because she disappeared into the kitchen.

He moved in close to Alessandra again, tossing his hat on a nearby hook before he reached for her. One hand cupped her shoulder while he threaded his other hand through the hair at her nape, feeling for a bump.

Crap. The sweater was as soft as it looked. And her hair was even softer.

"I'm sorry if I hurt you." He said the words more to distract himself than anything else.

It didn't work.

"I'll be all right." From this close, her softly-spoken words were only a puff of air against his chin. "I thought I was safe here."

He didn't feel a bump or abrasion on the back of her head, but for some reason his hand got stuck there, cupping the back of her head like a boyfriend might hold a girlfriend.

He read the questions and lingering fear in her expressive eyes. "I got a call from one of my buddies and there's still some noise that your family remains a target. I don't have any evidence that someone is *here*, but..."

Her lip trembled, slightly. And for a prolonged moment, he really wanted to lean in and kiss her. Wanted it so bad that he let go of her completely and stepped back, so quickly that she wobbled and had to steady herself with one hand against the wall.

What was he even thinking? He was sweaty and smelled like horses from working out in the barn. He was probably the last person on earth that she'd be interested in kissing.

"I don't know..." He turned his back and ran a hand through his hair again. What was it about her that shook him up so badly? "It could be nothing, but I've got a feeling. Like something's coming."

He dared to look at her, hoping he wouldn't see an expression that meant she thought he was crazy.

She didn't. She looked slightly steadier than she had earlier, her eyes more clear.

"We don't know each other very well, but I trust you," she said. "If you want me to take more precautions, I will. Although I haven't stepped foot outside since yesterday. Until..." She nodded to the door, and he remembered the feeling of her pressed against him on the other side of that wall. Remembered too well.

And the fear that had caused it.

He nodded. "I appreciate it." He couldn't let himself think about something happening to her.

Alessandra relied on every stitch of media training she'd ever had to present a calm facade as she preceded Gideon into the kitchen.

He'd been frightened when he'd barreled into her outside. She'd felt it in the intentionality of his compact movements.

It was hard to imagine what might frighten someone like Gideon, who was so very much a soldier, so sure of himself. That in itself was scary.

That fear remained with her now.

Whether the danger was real or not, he'd shielded her completely. She'd been under a protective detail hundreds of times, but she'd never had she felt so totally safe.

And then, in the mudroom... She'd thought for a moment that he would kiss her.

She'd wanted him to. Wanted to know what it felt like to be kissed by someone as virile and alive as Gideon.

Oh, she'd had a few first kisses. The rare second one. The men her father would approve of were groomed and polished. Boring. She dealt with political and social issues on a daily basis. Didn't want her dating life to revolve around them.

Until now, she hadn't known what she'd been missing.

If she'd been braver, she might've used the opportunity to stretch up on tiptoes and kiss *him*. But she'd chickened out.

All Gideon had seen from her was a scared rabbit, one who knew how to clean. So what? He hadn't seen how eloquent she could be. Hadn't seen her passion for children—her mostly-secret passion, as she didn't have enough time to devote to the charities she really wanted to help.

He'd probably rebuff her if she got up the courage

to kiss him.

He stopped short in the kitchen, hanging back where the bright lights changed from the mudroom and hallway to the kitchen proper.

Carrie was at the stove, stirring the pot of chili they'd worked on together earlier. Alessandra could hear Scarlett giving some of the hands a preschool lesson in the dining room.

But it was Dan and Trey that Gideon was staring at. As if he'd never seen them before. "What—?"

Both men were clean shaven, and Carrie had given them both haircuts before supper. They looked completely different—in fact, Alessandra had startled at first when she'd walked into the hall and spotted Trey earlier. They even wore button-up shirts over their jeans that seemed to be freshly laundered. In the dining room, she'd seen that Brian and Chase had done the same.

"I brought my shears out from the shop this afternoon. They clean up pretty good, don't they?" Carrie asked. She patted Trey—nearest her—on the shoulder.

Alessandra looked between the Trey and Gideon, who seemed to be having some kind of stare-off contest.

"Any reason you pokes decided to get all gussied up? Today?" There was a slightly menacing tone in

Gideon's words, one that would have had her cowering in her shoes if it had been aimed at her.

But Trey's chin jerked even higher. "Pretty ladies coming around makes a man want to look his best, boss."

"Maybe the *ladies* won't be hanging around for long," Gideon growled.

Carrie crossed her arms over her chest, aiming a glance that was almost belligerent toward her brother. "*I* think it's about time."

Gideon made an incoherent sound beneath his breath, and Alessandra had to pinch her lips together to keep from smiling. Carrie had told her earlier that her big brother was overprotective, but Alessandra hadn't gotten to see it in action until now. She couldn't help but wonder at the interplay among Gideon, his sister, and Trey.

Dan had wisely slipped into the dining room when he'd seen Gideon's thunderous expression.

"What about you, Gideon?" Carrie asked, her words almost a taunt. She used the first two fingers of one hand to make a clipping motion. "How long has it been since you've had a cut?"

Gideon shot an inscrutable look in Alessandra's direction before he shook his head tightly at his sister. "Not tonight."

"Gideon's probably hungry," Alessandra put in,

wanting to ease the strange tension that had built at Carrie's last comment. "He didn't come in for lunch."

She moved to dish him a deep bowl of chili, nudging Carrie out of the way. The other woman slipped her arm through Trey's, and they escaped into the front hall, bypassing the dining room. The cadence of their low conversation carried, but not the actual words.

"You don't have to cook for us," he said, shouldering in next to her and running water to scrub his hands in the sink.

The scent of sharp spices rose to her as she ladled out the meat and beans.

"And I don't have to clean for you," she returned, holding out the bowl and a spoon upright for him. "It makes me feel useful."

He finished drying his hands and tucked the towel back in its holder above the sink. One eyebrow quirked. "You have a hard time relaxing? Ever go on vacation?"

A slow blush burned her cheeks, but she met his gaze squarely. She was used to her life being scheduled. Tightly packed with activities. It wasn't anything to be ashamed of. "Sometimes it's easier to stay busy."

He couldn't know how true it was, especially when living with her father and older sister. The truth was, she'd felt more affection from the cowboys and Carrie here than she had in years with her own family. Being on the Triple H felt like *home.*

So cleaning up a little and cooking didn't feel like chores. It felt like giving back to the people who'd helped her, who'd made her feel welcome.

~ * ~

For the second night in a row, Alessandra couldn't sleep. Not only did she have to contend with the images of Tim's death, but now there was the worry of someone coming after her here, on Gideon's land. After the boisterous supper and some visiting with the cowboys before bedtime, once everything had quieted, she couldn't forget those moments with Gideon's on the back porch.

She'd run to save her life, but had she managed to put Gideon and his family's and employees' lives in danger?

She crept down to the first floor, once again to the cadence of snoring cowboys in the upstairs hallway.

But this time, when she hit the bottom step, an arm like an iron band wrapped around her waist, and a hand clamped over her mouth.

She panicked and a shriek rose in her throat. Would anyone even hear her with her mouth and nose blocked?

"Ssh."

The hand moved away from her mouth, while the arm remained.

She opened her mouth to scream when the man's scent and presence registered. *Gideon.*

Heart thrumming like a hummingbird's wings, she struggled to draw breath. Her knees weak from fright, the band of his arm was the only thing holding her upright.

He whispered a rough word. "I didn't mean to scare you. Matt's just outside the back door. I think he's on the phone. I was trying to hear his conversation."

She panted through the pounding of her heart but couldn't manage to catch her breath.

He seemed to realize exactly how shaken up she was, because he gently turned her toward him, though the embrace was loose, with space between their bodies. "Sorry," he murmured. "Sorry."

One of his hands came up to cup her cheek, his chapped skin warm against her chilled self.

"Alessandra..."

He breathed her name—her real name. It was the first time she'd heard it since she'd been on the ranch. And then, as if he couldn't help himself, he bent his head toward her and kissed her.

Earlier, she'd wondered what it would feel like to be kissed by Gideon. The reality was like being swept away in a tsunami. Blood rushed to her face at the first brush of his lips against hers. His mouth slanted gently but firmly against hers as his nose brushed her cheek. She'd expected his beard to feel stiff and bristly, but instead it was soft, his mustache tickling her upper lip. She smiled into the kiss, and he drew away slightly, leaving only a breath between their lips.

She brushed his upper lip with her index finger. Whispered, "I've never kissed a man with a beard before."

She was close enough to make out the slight flare of his nostrils before he lowered his head to hers once more. This time he deepened the kiss, and she was lost in a wave of swirling warmth.

Too soon, he drew away, pressing his cheek against hers.

"Sorry," this time he breathed the word against her cheek.

Sorry for scaring her, or for kissing her?

Her trembling had steadied, but now her body hummed with something else entirely. "I thought..." She tried to speak, but her voice emerged wobbly. "I thought someone had gotten inside."

He moved slightly away, holding her loosely now. He used one hand to brush a strand of hair out of her face. "No one's going to get inside. Apollo would sound an alert."

She heard the dog's snuffle of a snore from somewhere else in the house. Maybe from near the front door?

"He didn't bark when I came downstairs," she pointed out.

She sensed more than saw him smile in the dark. "I asked the hands to set up a watch. Someone'll be awake at all times during the night. Nobody's getting inside. Matt's on first."

She exhaled a breath that was slightly less shaky. "Why were you spying on your brother?"

She felt tension through the links of his arms still around her. She still couldn't see his face. There was a long pause before he answered. "I think something is wrong. Maybe it's a woman or maybe something happened just before he got sent home on leave."

"Have you asked him about it?" It was a terribly impertinent question, but it slipped out anyway.

"Tried," came the short answer. "He's not being real forthcoming."

"How sure are you?"

If anything, the tension in him increased. "It's nothing I can put my finger on. Just a..."

"Feeling." She waited for him to say something more, but he remained silent. So she offered, "Maybe he'll open up when he's ready."

She couldn't see Gideon's face, but could almost imagine the skeptical twist of his lips, though he didn't make a sound.

"He's an adult," she whispered, feeling as if she were stepping over the line with the statement. But it was true. It was admirable that Gideon cared what was going on with his brother, but Matt didn't have to tell his brother anything. It—whatever it was—was his burden to bear.

Gideon didn't respond, and she was afraid she *had* overstepped.

Then he shook her slightly. "There's nothing left for you to clean. You should be sleeping."

"I haven't tackled the living room windows yet," she teased softly. Then, in a whisper. "I...can't sleep. Every time I start to drift off, I see..." *Tim.*

His hands tightened infinitesimally where they rested on her waist.

She swallowed hard. "My...my mom died when I was young, but I don't really remember..."

A breath passed between them.

"This was different," he said, and his voice was rough. "It was violent. Traumatic."

She nodded, throat closing up.

"It will take some time. The memories will start to lose their power. You won't forget, but the sharpness of those moments will fade. You'll be able to divert your thoughts. Sleep better."

"Really?" She could barely fathom it.

"Yeah." He must've sensed that she needed extra reassurance because he went on. "One of the first missions I went on... We were sent in covertly to rescue this hostage. Our cover was blown."

She could tell from the deepening timber of his voice that it was hard for him to talk about this. She rested her palms gently against his muscled chest, wanting to offer comfort. She was more than a little impressed by the strength she felt beneath her hands.

"We got out, but the hostage was shot. He bled out in my hands. I didn't sleep for a week. Spent some time talking to the shrink assigned to the Teams. Still had trouble turning it off, but after awhile...it got easier."

His story ended, and she could hear the rough breaths as he exhaled. She couldn't see his face—no doubt he was thankful for that—but she still knew that re-telling these events had reopened the wound he felt. Because there was more to the man this his gruff, powerful demeanor.

"Thank you for telling me," she said. It seemed so inadequate for what he'd given her.

Knowing that a strong, powerful man like Gideon was, in fact, as human as she was a comfort. It likely wouldn't help her to sleep tonight, or tomorrow night, but she was glad he'd shared with her.

"Is that why you're worried about Matt? Are you afraid something like that happened to him?"

He exhaled, the puff of warm air brushing her forehead. "I guess. After what happened during my last tour—my stepdad died—now it's up to me to take care of the family."

It was a nice thought, but... Matt and Carrie were adults, each with their own lives. The ranch was well-run, with a foreman and plenty of hands. Was Gideon's sense of caretaking verging on overprotective?

She didn't know the whole situation. Had only known Gideon for two days. How could she make a judgment? She couldn't.

Suddenly the back door opened, and there was the sound of motion as Matt must have stepped inside. "Gid?"

Gideon cleared his throat. "Yeah."

The kitchen light flipped on, and Gideon stepped away from Alessandra, his arms finally falling away.

"Uh... am I interrupting something?" Matt's voice wasn't loud, but it carried a definite note of amusement.

"No," Gideon said firmly. Although if Matt had come in minutes earlier, he definitely would've been interrupting. "Allie can't sleep, and I thought I'd take her with me out to the barn."

Matt stared at his brother, an enigmatic expression crossing his face.

"Not for too long," Gideon insisted.

Matt shrugged. "This is your mission, brother. Do what you want."

Glad she'd pulled on a pair of jeans and warm, woolen socks with the long-sleeved T-shirt she'd worn to bed, Alessandra followed Gideon to the mudroom as Matt changed places with them, arms crossed over his chest as he watched from the hallway.

"You can borrow one of mine, even though it'll swallow you up." Gideon pulled a heavy brown corduroy coat from a hook on the wall and held it open for her. She stuffed her arms in the sleeves. Her hands didn't even poke through the ends, and the coat hung past her thighs.

He tugged, turning her back toward him, before he looped a scratchy knitted scarf over her neck and began tucking the front ends in a loose knot.

"Um..." She lifted her right foot to show the woolen socks.

His mouth quirked. "We've got an old pair of Carrie's boots here." He bent, rifling among the boots lined up against the wall, finally coming up with a pair of what looked like a cross between rain boots and work boots. "They might be a little big."

She had to hold onto his shoulder as he helped her step into the boots. And if she held on a moment too long, well...who could blame her?

CHAPTER SEVEN

Gideon knew this was a bad idea. Spending time alone with Alessandra. Getting close to her.

Definitely kissing her had been a bad idea.

But he couldn't seem to help himself, not when she'd been shaken by the memories of what had happened to her in New York. He knew what that was like.

And...okay. His motives weren't entirely altruistic.

The more time he spent with her, the more he liked her. She was a good listener. Didn't tell him he was foolish to be spying on his brother.

Getting involved with someone who was leaving felt like the most dangerous thing he'd done since he'd left the Teams.

But he couldn't seem to help himself.

He hustled her across the expanse of yard between the house and barn. *If* someone was watching the place, they probably wouldn't be expecting to see the princess coming outside at this time of night. And he'd bundled her up pretty good.

It only took seconds to jog across the space with Alessandra tucked under his arm, and then they reached the barn.

"You'll want to keep your coat on," he cautioned as he pulled the door closed. Although the building offered the protection from the cutting wind, only the office was heated, and not by much.

She followed him in, looking all around, her face open with curiosity and wonder. Her nose wrinkled adorably.

"You don't like the smell?" he teased.

"Now I understand why all the cowboys have been heading for the shower first thing before supper," she retorted. She smiled. *Smiled!* "It's the scent of your trade," she said with a little shrug. "It isn't disgusting."

He didn't know about that. "Glad you think so, but I'd still advise watching your step."

"What do you do out here at night?" she asked. "Aren't the animals sleeping?"

He led the way to the plank fence that separated them from the open part of the barn, where a mama and her new baby did, in fact, sleep. Opposite, a second cow circled in an agitated manner. Her belly was distended and judging by her movements, she was close.

"It's calving season." He motioned her to join him at the railing. "Right now we've got several new babies being born every day." He leveled a look at her. "And some at night. We track the cows that are close and try to get them into the barn, so we can watch them and make sure there aren't any complications with the birth."

"Are there often complications?"

He shrugged. "Sometimes. We help out if we can, get the vet out here if it turns into an emergency situation." He nodded to the cow who had now lain in the hay. "This little lady looks like she's close. If I'm right, you can watch a little miracle."

She leaned both elbows on the railing. Her hands weren't visible in the coat at all, it swallowed her up. But he'd felt a visceral *Mine!* when he'd tucked her into the coat a few minutes earlier.

"It seems like a lot of sleepless night," she said with a sideways glance at him.

"For about a month. Maybe six weeks." He shrugged. "It's part of running a cattle operation."

"It must be vastly different than what you used to do—in the military."

He nodded. "It is. More cyclical. A lot less training required."

But she didn't seem to appreciate his humor. "Do you ever miss it? Being on assignment? Going into danger?"

Being on high alert this week had certainly reminded him of what he'd left behind. He missed being an important part of the team, having a critical assignment that meant the life or death of the mission.

"Doesn't matter. My knee blew out on my last mission. I wouldn't be fit for active duty anymore." And that killed him. He kept his focus on the cow, aware of Alessandra's gaze on his face. The cow was straining, obviously in the throes of labor, but nothing seemed to be happening.

"Besides," he said offhandedly, "someone's got to run this place. And Carrie and the squirt need me."

She slanted a look at him. "It seems as if Trey might be angling for the *she-needs-me* position in Carrie's life."

He grunted. "He'd better not be."

"Why not? He works for you. You've got to have some trust in him." Her statement was innocent, but it didn't help the acid churning in his gut.

"After what happened to her, Carrie needs someone..." He searched for the right word, but it wasn't coming to him easily.

"Who makes a better living than a cowhand?" she asked, turning to face him. "Who's more trustworthy? Good-looking? From a better background?"

He matched her stance, looking right down on her. "None of those."

Her head tilted to the side. "Then what?"

He ran a hand over his beard. "Two years ago, while I was on my last mission, my uncle died. Carrie's ex-husband had been gone since before Scarlett was born. But all of a sudden, he showed up. Thought she stood to get a big inheritance and tried to pound it out of her. By the time he was done, she had a concussion, broken arm, and two busted ribs."

It still made him sick to think about it. He'd been gone, and Carrie had been helpless.

Alessandra touched him, cupped his elbow in one hand. Brought him back from that dark place when he'd been laid up in the hospital, barely able to move for his knee, knowing nobody was there to take care of his sister.

"I think it's admirable that you want to be there for Carrie, but..." She bit her lip, looking down. "She is a grown woman. She can date—or marry—whomever she wants."

He knew that. He just wanted her to pick a winner this time. And while he'd known Trey for years, he wasn't sure the hand was the right guy for his sister.

He looked back to the cow, saw she was still in distress. "I've got to go in there and check her out."

~ * ~

Alessandra watched Gideon hop the fence and move to the cow lying prostrate in the hay.

"So now you've got the dish about Carrie. I want to know why your aunt is targeting your family."

She shivered, burrowing deeper into the coat. "I've never met my aunt, and my father doesn't like to talk about her."

"They don't get along?" He'd approached the cow's *derriere* and squatted there. From where she stood, she couldn't see exactly what he was doing.

"My father has...some challenges. It isn't publicized, but he's battled MS for years. It's terminal, and he's getting worse every day."

A few moments passed as he looked over the cow.

"That must be hard," he finally said.

It was. More so because she wanted things to be different. She'd hoped that being faced with his mortality would mean that her father would spend more time with her and her sisters. That she could get to know the *man* and not the *king*.

But instead, he'd pushed each of the three girls to work harder for the kingdom in the name of family duty. He'd insisted on carrying out his duties as much as possible. Because most of the burden of her father's illness fell on Eloise, Alessandra often felt invisible to her father.

There was a rush of fluid and blood and a little black body plopped into the hay near Gideon's feet. Gideon reached for clumps of hay and began rubbing, drying the little body.

The calf floundered in the hay for moments, and then mama and baby both managed their feet, and Gideon backed slowly away.

He returned to where she stood, hopping the fence again and standing elbow-to-elbow with her at the railing.

Although he watched as the mama licked her baby all over, she knew Gideon's attention was still focused on her.

"What about your security team?" Gideon asked. "Have there been any heightened threats lately? Phone calls to the palace? Letters?"

She was ashamed that she didn't know. "Not that I've been briefed on."

"No ex-boyfriends with an agenda?"

She turned her head to meet his sideways glance straight on. "No ex-boyfriends." She'd had dates, sometimes multiple dates, but no one serious enough to call a boyfriend.

Had he asked out of concern about the shooting, or was he fishing?

She raised her brows at him. "What about you?

Did your last girlfriend break your heart? There's no one special for you?"

He frowned, eyes on the cow and calf. "I didn't date while on the Teams. It's hard on girlfriends not to know where your man is or if he'll come back. Hang on."

He went back into the pen, approaching the mama and baby slowly.

The cow bellowed at him, and he froze a few feet in.

"What's wrong?" she whispered.

"The calf should be suckling by now," he answered over his shoulder. "She's not helping it out. And she doesn't seem to want to let me get close."

He didn't elaborate. He attempted to get close to the animals twice more, but the cow lowered its head when he neared, and he backed off, returned to the fence near Alessandra.

She'd seen that thundercloud expression on his face before.

"What will happen, then?" Alessandra worried aloud. "Will the calf—?"

"If she rejects it, we'll likely end up bottle-feeding the thing. Which is a huge pain."

His focus was still on the animals, and he didn't see the twitch of her lips.

He might be gruff, but she was learning to see

beyond it. He was soft enough to care if the calf lived or died, and not just for the money. He might complain about having to feed the calf, but she knew he would do it.

He was just that kind of cowboy.

CHAPTER EIGHT

Over the next few days, Gideon watched as Alessandra seem to thrive in ranch life.

With no further sign of anyone on their property, no noise from local law enforcement, and Cash assuring him that the reports they were getting didn't have Alessandra's whereabouts located anywhere near north Texas, he no longer kept her confined to the house.

She spent hours in the barn, bottle-feeding the calf she'd dubbed Valentine.

She cooked and cleaned up after the hands, no matter how much he chided her to do otherwise. Where, before her arrival, the hands had been rowdy and willing to let their appearance and behavior slide, they were more polite and cleaned up each night before supper. She'd changed them for the better.

Once, he caught her watching a national news broadcast with a pensive look on her face, but other than that, she seemed content.

He, however, was a boiling mess of emotions.

He couldn't seem to keep himself from sneaking kisses. In the barn. After supper, while she corralled him to dry dishes for her. He found her addictive, especially when she smiled a secret little smile after he'd kissed her—a smile he hadn't seen her give to anyone else.

He'd even trimmed his beard. He hadn't shaved it, because she seemed to like it.

But all the while, he reminded himself that she wasn't here to stay, no matter how well she seemed to fit into his life.

She was used to the jet-set lifestyle. Fancy parties. Events where she rubbed elbows with famous people.

She would eventually marry a prince.

Not an ex-Navy SEAL with a ruined knee and obligations that tied him to the family ranch.

Somehow, he'd become uncomfortable in his own life as well. He needed to keep Alessandra safe. He'd accepted it as his own personal mission. So he left Nate with more responsibility, so he could scout their land and the neighbors close by.

Though he'd relaxed a little, allowing Alessandra to the barn, he didn't trust that things had gone quiet. Every so often, he got that awful feeling down the back of his neck and shoulders, like someone was watching.

Waiting.

Biding their time.

Like he'd do, if he was tasked with taking out the princess.

It just made him more itchy, being out of the loop. Relying on the Glorvaird and New York enforcement agencies. Not being in on it.

And he wasn't a patient man.

Even through his distraction, the Triple H hadn't fallen down around their shoulders.

Was Matt right that Gideon had stunted Nate's potential by taking on too much responsibility for the ranch duties?

Worse, was Alessandra right that he'd done the same to Carrie? Had he kept his little sister from finding happiness because he'd been determined to fix every single thing that went wrong in her life?

He didn't know how to manage all of that.

He didn't know how to keep from getting hurt when Alessandra left. Where his place was, if it wasn't as the boss of the Triple H. Who needed him, if Carrie didn't? If he couldn't help Matt? If Nate could run the ranch without him?

He was anchorless. A SEAL without a team.

And then his phone rang.

~ * ~

Alessandra felt Gideon's heightened tension at supper. Almost as if he was pulling away from her.

After the meal, he drew her into the living room, leaving Matt and the hands behind at the dining table.

His expression was deadly serious as he said, "Your head of security called. They're ready for you to come home to Glorvaird."

She'd known it was coming, but the words were still unexpected. She wasn't ready yet. Valentine was only a few days old. And she was supposed to have lunch with Carrie on Friday.

And Gideon...

He was already heading for the door. "You'll want to pack up tonight. We'll leave early in the morning for the airport. They're sending you a new passport, which we'll pick up on the way."

And then he was gone, banging through the mudroom and out the back door.

She sat for a moment, heart pounding. Should she follow him?

She'd give him until the dishes were done to clear his mind.

But he didn't come back, not after the last dish had been washed and put away.

She waited in the living room, curled beneath an afghan as the house darkened around her. She let her eyes roam, noting the changes. She and Carrie had made them together. Photos of the Hales: Gideon, Matt, Carrie, and Scarlett, now lined the walls. A pitcher with hothouse flowers from town claimed space on the end table.

It wasn't the empty dreary room it had been when she'd arrived.

She'd like to think she'd brought changes to the people, too.

She idly played with the phone Gideon had given her, scanning through the pictures on the high-tech device. She'd surreptitiously taken several candid photos of Gideon when he hadn't been watching. Him working with the cattle, actively shooing two mama cows and their days-old babies back out into the open pasture. Laughing from across the supper table at something Matt had said. She rarely saw those genuine smiles cross Gideon's face, much less his entire face lit and open with laughter. Mostly when he interacted with his family, though a few times his expression had been open and soft after they'd kissed.

She traced the line of his smile with the tip of her finger. She was falling in love with the irascible cowboy.

She'd thought something real was growing between them. Which was why his absence tonight confused and hurt her.

At ten, she decided not to wait any longer. She was a princess, wasn't she? Capable of standing up for herself. Facing hard things, not cowering. She'd find Gideon and tell him how she felt. They couldn't leave things like this. Unresolved.

All the cowhands were upstairs in bed, except for Nate, who nursed a cup of coffee as he stood in front of the kitchen window, looking out.

She'd already bundled up in the heaviest sweater Carrie had loaned her and thick wool socks. "I'm going to run out to the barn," she told the hand, whose eyes twinkled with merriment.

"I'll keep an eye out," he promised.

She slipped into Carrie's old work boots and Gideon's coat, bundling up as best she could before she darted across the yard.

Something felt different tonight.

She was aware of Nate standing on the back porch, watching her cross to the barn. But somehow, without Gideon beside her, the darkness felt menacing. The cold felt threatening.

Was her mind making things up because of the anticipation of leaving tomorrow? She'd found safety, an inkling of peace on the ranch.

Wind rushed at her back, and she misjudged the final few feet, running into the door with a *thump*. She straightened, not hurt but a little shaken at the way she'd let her imagination take off. When she tugged on the door, it wouldn't budge.

And then it did, almost ripping from her hands. Gideon stood there, inches from her.

His face was dark as he pulled her inside the lit space, throwing a glare over her shoulder.

"What the—?" He mumbled what she thought was an expletive before releasing her. She reeled a few feet away. "You walked out here in the dark, alone?"

"I ran," she said. "And Nate was watching from the porch. Besides... aren't you taking the bodyguard thing a little far? I thought things were safe now."

He muttered something else beneath his breath. "Just because nothing's happened doesn't mean you're safe. It could mean the threat has gone underground."

It was a valid point. She'd had no sense that anything had been wrong in New York City, either. Gideon was the soldier.

"I'm sorry."

Her apology didn't seem to ease his tension. His Stetson was pulled low over his eyes, and he backed a few feet farther from her.

She wrapped her arms around her middle under the pretense of holding the coat together. "If you'd come inside earlier, I wouldn't have had to come looking for you."

"Shouldn't you be in bed by now?" he muttered.

"Shouldn't you?" she returned. Then, softer, "I need to talk to you."

"Why?" he asked, voice flat. "Why are we still pretending when you're going home tomorrow?"

His words stung. "Pretending?" It had all been real to her. Every moment with Gideon had brought a sense of belonging.

Until now.

"I can't do it anymore." The hardness in his voice was like being struck, and she clutched herself tighter. "Pretend that all of this is going to have a happy ending."

A muscle ticked away in his jaw, proving he wasn't as emotionless as he let on.

She took a deep breath, searching for the right words.

"I've been doing some thinking," she said, heart thrumming loudly in her ears. "We might come from different places, but that doesn't mean we can't be together—"

He laughed, a harsh sound. "Are you going to ditch your family and stay on the ranch? I know you've been enjoying yourself, but what about Dear Old Dad? What about your *obligations*?" His words were a verbal punch. She'd confided in him that she often felt stifled by her royal duties. That she wished for a closer relationship with her father. And now he was throwing her words back at her.

She shivered at the twist of his lips. Why was he being this way?

"You know I wouldn't be able to stay on all time. But if we split our time—"

"Split our time?"

She jerked her chin up. "You are more than the Triple H. You're well spoken and intelligent. Well-traveled. You could hold your own with any of the dignitaries I've met."

He looked dumbfounded. "You want me to go with you?"

"Like I said, we could split our time—"

But he was already shaking his head. "I can't leave. I've got to be here to look after the ranch—"

"That's Nate's job," she reminded him softly. She could see from the set of his shoulders that she wasn't getting through.

"What if something happened to Carrie again, and I was half the globe away?"

And she could see the guilt eating him up, still.

"What if you were half the globe away, and *nothing*

happened?" she asked gently. "What if you're giving up your chance at a different life for a hypothetical?"

He took off his hat and ran his hand through his hair, a gesture she knew meant he was upset.

"My whole life has been planned out for me, up until now," she said, wishing, praying that he could understand. "I never had a reason to fight for anything different, until now. Until you."

Hat still clutched in one hand, he looked at her. She could see the torment in his eyes. "I just don't see how it would work, long-term."

"But..." *She loved him.* The words stuck in her throat at the resigned look on his face.

"It makes sense that the ranch has been a place of rest for you. Something totally different than what you're used to. And a place that's kept you safe. But in six months, or next year during calving season... the newness will wear off. Even if you split your time..."

She noticed he didn't use the word *we*.

"You'll figure out this place is all work, work, and more *work*. *We*"—he pointed back and forth between them—"won't work. Not for long."

She didn't know how he'd become so defeated. Did he really think they were that different, after all she'd tried to do to prove to him that she could be a cowgirl, too?

Tears rose, and she valiantly fought them back. Her heart might be breaking, but she didn't want him to see, not now that he'd rejected her.

"I'll see you home," he said, and she couldn't look at him. "But that's it. That's all it can be."

~ * ~

Gideon wasn't his best self the next morning, not after tossing and turning for hours.

He couldn't erase the image of Alessandra holding herself together last night, her hands shaking as she clutched her elbows.

As if, by denying that they could have something lasting together, he'd broken her.

The SEALs had taught him the value of considering every angle, every scenario, every possible ending. He couldn't see a way forward that didn't end with one of them in heartbreak—most likely him.

He feared his heart might be breaking now. He felt nauseated, like something he'd eaten last night hadn't set well with him.

She'd been quiet on the ride to Dallas, once again sandwiched between him and Matt in the truck. He'd spent the entire drive watching for a tail, unconvinced she was safe, and fighting the icy roads.

There was no tail, but he still had that awful feeling down the back of his neck.

The airport was bustling as he pulled into the underground parking lot where this had all started. She slid out of the truck after him, and when as he helped her to the ground, he got his first good look at her of the morning. She wore a long, elegant coat similar to the one she'd worn that very first day. It fell open, revealing a slim pantsuit and heels— though not as unwieldy as the stone-encrusted ones they'd found her in. She looked night-and-day different from the farm girl who'd worn her hair in a braid and donned one of his flannel shirts when she fed the undernourished calf. Carrie must've gone shopping on her behalf, though they still hadn't let his sister in on "Allie's" secret identity.

He and Matt flanked her as they walked inside.

"Keep your eyes open," he told his brother, though it wasn't necessary. At least Matt seemed to be taking this seriously, scanning the crowds as they passed through the lower-level corridor and then arrived at the passenger check-in. Because Gideon had printed her boarding pass at home, they were able to move directly to the Security line. He'd coordinated with the royal security team and planned to accompany her to New York, then hop a flight right back home. Matt would kill time around here, and they'd drive back to the Triple H together.

This was the end of his time with Alessandra.

She hugged Matt at the Security line, then walked through, that princess-grace evident in her posture, her calm exterior.

Gideon stayed close, silent, like a bodyguard would. Which felt appropriate, since she still wasn't speaking to him.

She clutched his cell phone between her hands, though he didn't know why.

Inside the terminal, they discovered the flight had been delayed as the airport personnel de-iced the runway. He growled quietly. It was only an hour's delay, but it meant more time out in the open.

The hair on the back of his neck was tingling again, this time the pit of his stomach carried a knot the size of a boulder.

The gate attendant confirmed the delay, and he stifled the urge to punch someone.

"Can we get something to eat?" the princess asked.

He agreed reluctantly.

Everyone else seemed to have the same idea, because the few food places that were open on their end of the terminal were packed. Alessandra stood in line for a bakery kiosk, him beside her.

The feeling on the back of his neck got worse. He

kept Alessandra close to his side, noticing and hating it when she unobtrusively put a few inches between them.

He craned his neck, trying to see in all directions. Could someone have snuck a gun inside the airport, where security was tight? Or a knife? He knew it could happen, but...

There. Near the restrooms, a man in a long trench coat was darting looks in all directions, one hand tucked beneath his coat. Gideon lost focus on the crowd around them as he zeroed in on the suspicious guy.

"Sorry the lines are so long," an older, feminine voice said from nearby. "Would you like to try one of our apple fritters? It's a free sample."

Gideon turned back to the princess, just in time to see her take a paper-wrapped pastry from a uniformed woman. He didn't get a good look at the woman's face, only the dingy gray ponytail hanging from the back of her ballcap.

Focus now split between Trench-coat Guy and the woman who'd approached Alessandra, Gideon lost a half-second of reaction time.

"Wait—"

But he was too late to stop the princess from raising the tissue-wrapped pastry to her mouth. She ate a bite.

Still distracted by Trench-coat Guy, he put his hand beneath Alessandra's elbow. "Can we sit down now?" He didn't wait for an answer.

They didn't make it back.

"Gideon, I'm—"

Alessandra faltered mid-step, and the only reason he was able to catch her around the waist was because he'd been so close to her.

What was happening?

Her eyelids fluttered rapidly, and her cheeks were reddening as he watched. She collapsed, and the pastry she'd held dropped to the floor.

Panic threading through his veins, he knelt, cradling her head. "Alessandra. Honey?"

He searched for a pulse even as she lost consciousness.

"Help!" he called out, waving down the gate attendant. "I need medical help!"

He touched her beneath the coat, feeling for any sign of a bullet entry, though there was no blood blooming, and he'd heard no *pop*, even from a gunshot that had been silenced.

Had she been poisoned? The thought was absurd, but what else could've happened?

Fear clawed through him at her weak, fluttering pulse.

He was supposed to have protected her.

How could he have let this happen?

CHAPTER NINE

Hours later, Gideon sat beside Alessandra's hospital bed in the secure ICU wing of the university hospital, head in his hands.

He'd been praying, frantic wordless prayers, since the princess had been poisoned at the airport. He'd believed the royal security team when they'd said the danger was past. Hadn't given enough credence to his gut.

Someone had gotten close enough to *poison* her.

And Gideon had let it happen.

The doctors had praised his quick thinking as he'd scooped up the remainder of the apple pastry into a plastic baggie before they'd rushed Alessandra out of the airport on a medevac helicopter. First, they'd pumped her stomach. Initial testing of the pastry had identified large doses of cyanide, and the doctors had quickly given her an anti-cyanide antidote kit.

She'd remained unconscious since the airport. It was probably a blessing for her not to be awake to feel the poison ravaging her body, but Gideon wished and prayed for nothing more than her to open those bright blue eyes and look at him.

He pinched the bridge of his nose, hoping to stem the tears that burned behind his nose.

In all the chaos, with his adrenaline pumping, he'd felt the same clarity he had back when he was with the Teams on a mission. The high-octane situation had burned away all his excuses, all the worries that had once seemed so important that they'd clouded his judgment. And his true feelings.

He loved her.

And all the rest of it didn't matter.

She'd been right. They could figure things out with their schedules, the ranch, his siblings.

None of that mattered when all he could see was her closed eyes, her motionless body.

He just wanted to *be* with her. For any time they could carve out to spend together, for now, forever.

But first, she had to wake up. The doctors and nurses were monitoring her closely, but they wouldn't be able to fully evaluate how much damage the cyanide had done until she regained consciousness.

A knock at the door brought his head up, though it felt as if it weighed a thousand pounds.

While the ER doctors had been working to save her life, he'd coordinated with local law enforcement and the nearest high-clearance security team he could find to set up this secure wing in the hospital. Where before he'd been content to let the royal security team manage things from offsite, he refused to risk her life again, not when he could do something about it.

Carrie stuck her head around the door, and he stood, surprise overcoming the lethargy in his limbs. "What're you doing here?"

"Matt called." She stepped inside as he reached for her, and her arms came around him in a hug that had him blinking against his burning eyes. "The guys are here, too, out in the waiting room."

He hugged her tightly, unable to find words. Alessandra had been right. He hadn't been able to protect her from right beside her. He needed to learn to let go and trust God and Carrie. She could handle her own life.

Even if it wasn't entirely comfortable right now.

"How is she?" Carrie asked.

"Unconscious." He ran a hand through his hair, missing his hat. It'd been lost somewhere in the melee. "It takes hours to run the full test on the poison she ingested, but the doctors think they've at least stopped it from doing further damage."

Carrie sniffled a little as she looked at Alessandra's pale face against the pillow, hair mussed and IVs trailing from Alessandra's arm.

Gideon's chest felt so full and hot that he wanted to howl.

Suddenly, more bodies were crowding inside. The ranch hands were led by Trey, who had his chin hitched in the air and a stubborn glint in his eyes. "Figured if y'all are holding a prayer vigil, we'd better all get in on it." He moved next to Carrie, one hand resting at her waist.

Gideon nodded once, letting the cowboy—and his friend—know that he couldn't protest a friendship or relationship anymore.

Matt came near, clapping him on the shoulder.

"The nurse know you're all in here? Probably against protocol." But for the moment, Gideon's will was too weak to protest more.

And then, Carrie and all the ranch hands had slung their arms around each other, circling the bed in one big man-hug as they bowed heads. On the end of the chain, Gideon gently laid his free hand on Alessandra's shoulder.

Each man shared a special prayer on Alessandra's behalf, beseeching God to heal her and bring her back to them.

By the time Dan had finished, every one of them was clearing his throat or surreptitiously wiping his eyes. They moved slightly away from each other and the brotherly intimacy of the moment, some of them shuffling their feet. Dan and Nate shoved their hats back on their heads.

"Is she really a princess?" Chase hooked his thumb over his shoulder.

Gideon glared at Matt, who raised his hands helplessly. "Sorry, man. Some reporter got shots while she was getting loaded into the helicopter."

Gideon winced.

"Got *pictures*," Matt corrected himself. "And by the time we got to the hospital, it was all over social media and local news stations."

That was a nightmare for another time. At least he'd had the foresight to secure this wing of the hospital.

"So she really is?" Chase pressed.

Gideon nodded. "Yeah."

Brian whistled low. "And we had her cleaning up after us like a maid."

Carrie's eyes were shining. "Scarlett will be thrilled. She's claimed this whole time that Allie was a princess."

Gideon rubbed the back of his neck with one hand. "She's not coming back to the Triple H. When she wakes up"—he almost choked on the words, but he had to believe she was going to wake up—"she's going back to Glorvaird."

Carrie looked at him with a glint of mischief in her eyes. "Maybe. I guess we'll see."

He clung to his sister's hope. Right now, it was all he had.

~ * ~

Alessandra was trapped in cold, terrifying darkness, unable to move. Barely able to think.

Voices came. Someone stuck something nasty down her throat and she gagged. The contents of her stomach emptied.

Oh, she *hated* being sick.

She was so hot.

No, *cold*.

And then came the voice of the man she loved. Gideon.

She even thought she heard Carrie, Matt, and the other hands. Were they...praying for her?

Peace and warmth stole over her. Snatches of conversation wafted to her, as if from far away.

"...she really a princess?"

"...she's going back to Glorvaird."

"Maybe..."

She couldn't go back. Not yet. There was still something undone. Something she hadn't told Gideon.

Why couldn't she wake up?

She needed...

She went cold again. Started shaking uncontrollably. Couldn't find her tongue.

And then there were voices again—strange ones. "She's seizing!"

Where had Gideon gone? Her friends?

She needed them.

Needed him.

Was lost.

~ * ~

It was after midnight, but Gideon couldn't sleep. The ICU room allowed for one uncomfortable chair, and the cowboys and his siblings had agreed to stay in the waiting room for now.

Why hadn't Alessandra woken?

Earlier, after the impromptu prayer vigil, she'd shown signs of improving.

And then she'd had some kind of seizure, her body reacting to the poison. The doctors had been able to help her ride it out, but since then, there'd been no sign of awareness behind her eyes. He imagined her lost in a deep pool. Maybe the seizure had brought her close to the surface. Since then, though, she seemed to have sunk all the way at the bottom, her beautiful heart hidden beneath the murky waves. Would she ever make it to the surface again?

Was he losing her? Was she drifting away even now as he watched her pale face?

This waiting...he was dying a slow death.

If she died, he would never be the same. He couldn't bear to think of a world where he wouldn't hear her laugh, see the flash of her teeth in that secret smile she'd only given to him.

He took her hand. Shook it gently. "Wake up, Allie-girl."

Nothing. No blip on the machines monitoring her. No catch of her breath.

"I need you—" His voice broke on the words. She'd never know how devastated he was at this moment, how very badly he'd realized he needed her.

"I was wrong. You were right." If ever there were words to wake a woman up...

And it was true. He'd been wrong to push her away. He should've been pulling her closer. They were a team, the two of them.

He waited. Still no change.

The clock ticked. The monitors proved she was still here, still with him. But still not.

"Please." He bowed his head over her hand, squeezed his eyes against the tears that were so close.

"Please." He didn't know what he was pleading for. For God not to take her, maybe. For her to come back to him.

Right now, thank you very much.

He rose from the chair, unable to contain the nervous energy that buzzed through him. He rested his hands against the railing and leaned over her, so pale and still in the bed. At least the awful red had faded from her skin, one of the signs of the cyanide poisoning.

"Alessandra," he breathed.

He leaned closer. Didn't even know what he was doing, but he had to do something.

He brushed one soft kiss, a feather kiss, again her mouth. One against her forehead. He let his chin rest against her temple.

And whispered, "I love you."

~ * ~

Alessandra felt Gideon's presence nearby, felt the brush of his whiskers against her temple.

"I love you."

She opened her eyes.

He froze. He backed slightly away, enough so she could see his dear face.

His hands were clamped around the hospital bed

railing, close enough that she barely had to move to reach for him. He met her grasp, his fingers tangling with hers.

"Alessandra." His breath caught, and there was no missing the sheen of tears in his eyes. Her sensitive *Bear.*

"Hi," she whispered, the word burning her throat. Tears stung her eyes.

He breathed out a shaky exhale, squeezed her hand once. He let go only to move away momentarily, and then he was back with a cup of water and a straw. He held it to her lips, and she drank greedily, feeling echoes of fever—or something—that had overwhelmed while she'd been lost in the darkness.

When she'd had her fill, he put away the cup. "I should call the nurse. There are a lot of people waiting for you to wake up."

He took her hand again and stared at her.

Long enough that she began to wonder what had happened. Had her hair been all shaved off? "What is it?"

He narrowed his eyes slightly. "For a bit there, I thought I might never see you looking back at me again."

"Was I sick?" she asked. "I remember feeling feverish, and cold. Choking. Throwing up."

"You were poisoned," he said. "You collapsed at the airport. The woman gave you that pastry... Remember?"

She did, barely.

"Mostly I remember you were going to let me walk away."

His eyes darkened, and he leaned close to touch his temple against hers. "That's because I was doing what my sex often does. Being an idiot."

Relief and love flowed through her. "So you've changed your mind, then? About us not *working* in the long-term?"

"Well, for one thing, your royal security team needs a massive overhaul. I can't trust them to get you back to Glorvaird safely, so it seems I'll be forced to accompany you at least that far."

He brushed a kiss against her upper cheek. "There's no telling how long it will take before they can be whipped into shape, and I can't leave you unprotected. You're too important." Though most of his words held a teasing note, those last were spoken with an intense seriousness.

"And then there's the fact that I've fallen in love with you," he said softly. "And I can't live without you. So I suppose the roundabout answer is: yes, I've changed my mind."

She raised her other hand, the first real movement

she'd made since waking. Everything seemed to be in working order, though she felt as weak as a baby. She cupped his cheek, his trimmed beard rough against her palm. "I'm in love with you, too."

His eyes squeezed shut, but not before she saw the depths of emotion that overwhelmed him.

"*That* seems like the second miracle of the day," he whispered. He brushed another gentle kiss against her lips. He drew away slightly, and her hand fell to the bed. "But if God wants to heap blessings on my head..."

She smiled. "You won't argue?"

"Not today."

He was forced to move back as a nurse and doctor bustled in, surprised to see her awake.

They began asking questions immediately, prodding her with a thermometer and stethoscope, but she held Gideon's gaze throughout.

It was a little bit astounding.

She'd never expected to be running for her life, then stranded on a working ranch for days on end. If not for New York, she never would have met Gideon.

Although he hadn't admitted to it, she guessed that if it hadn't been for Gideon's training and quick thinking, she could've died in the airport.

And then, he'd declared his love for her.

Miracles, indeed.

LACY WILLIAMS

EPILOGUE

"The Kissing Princess"

Mia, third in line to the Glorvaird crown, crumpled the newsprint between both hands.

She considered throwing it in the fire burning on the nearby hearth, but ultimately smoothed it out on the table. The headline shouted up at her again, making her lose any appetite for the breakfast spread laid out on a silver tray before her.

Is that what they really thought of her? All the public could see of her?

Beneath the headline was a photograph of her—yes, kissing—the young duke of Regis, a neighboring kingdom.

The long-range, slightly grainy photo didn't show the moments that followed, when she'd discovered his infidelity. The photograph didn't show the resounding slap she'd delivered.

The press liked to paint her as someone who hopped from boyfriend to boyfriend, who liked to

LACY WILLIAMS

play with men's hearts and give kisses freely, but it wasn't the truth. Not at all.

She fell in love easily. Too easily, as the line of jerks that had left her with a broken heart could attest to.

But the media didn't care about that.

Voices intruded, and she slouched in the wingback chair in the palace's blue parlor.

It sounded like her sister and her new— American—beau. She'd welcomed her sister back to the palace last night and met the handsome, dark-bearded man, but she didn't want company now. Maybe if she was quiet enough, still enough, they wouldn't find her here, and she could continue her sulk in private.

"You're having brunch with Eloise?" Gideon asked.

"Mm hmm. Worried about being left to your own devices?"

There was a quiet moment, and Mia squeezed her eyes closed, imagining her sister locking lips with the handsome American.

"Not too worried," came Gideon's voice, amused and warm. "I might sneak down and talk with your head of security while you're busy."

"Again?"

"There were a couple of recent email threats that

they should look into."

Mia's pulse sped momentarily. She'd been a part of the motorcade that the bombing had narrowly missed just three months ago. It had been the most frightening thing she'd ever experienced, and for brief seconds she'd thought she wouldn't survive. Since then, palace life had returned to a normal, if more vigilant, state.

She'd hoped that the threat was past, but it seemed Gideon didn't think so. Did he know something she didn't, or was his suspicion because of his former role as a soldier and the near-misses Alessandra had had?

"Stop *worrying* so much," Alessandra said to her beau. "You'll start to go prematurely gray, and then my people will think I'm dating a much older man."

"I'll stop *taking precautions* when I'm certain there are no threats against the woman I love."

It was a swoon-worthy statement. Mia's stomach twisted. Some of it was happiness for her sister. Some of it, she hated to admit, was envy. She wanted that kind of love for herself. Was desperate for it.

Her eyes fell to the front page again, as Alessandra and Gideon's voices faded to murmurs. Was it her imagination, or did her desperation show in the grainy photograph?

She couldn't go on like this. It wasn't healthy.

She needed to prove to herself—and to the kingdom—that she wasn't just the *kissing princess*.

And that's when she promised she would not kiss another man unless he was the man she would marry.

~ * ~

Gideon watched Alessandra disappear down the hall to meet her sister. He stood with both hands in the front pockets of his slacks, posture relaxed, just in case she turned around.

"I'll stop taking precautions when I'm certain there are no real threats against the woman I love."

He was fairly sure he'd convinced her that all he was thinking about was her security. Right now, nothing could be further from the truth.

When she turned the corner at the end of the opulent, marble-floored hall, he swiveled on his heel and marched back to the quarters he'd been assigned, in a different hall than where the princesses resided. He unrolled his shirt sleeves as he walked, pushing the cuffs back down and buttoning them.

He had another mission in mind today. And one didn't have an audience with the king in shirtsleeves. Inside the richly-appointed bedroom, he checked his black leather shoes for scuffs—none—and pulled the tie out of the top pocket of his suitcase, laid out on the foot of the bed.

Carrie had helped him pick it out. He'd confided in his sister before he and Alessandra had left the United States. She thought his plan to ask the king for Alessandra's hand before planning an extravagant proposal was romantic and perfect.

He wished he was as certain.

He stood before the bureau mirror, tucking the tie around his neck and knotting it.

In the past three months, he and Alessandra had been almost inseparable. He'd escorted her home a week after her near-fatal poisoning and met her older sister, Eloise. The king had been home, but the recent events had laid him up with an "episode," and Gideon hadn't had a chance to meet the man.

Gideon had stayed with Alessandra for nearly two months as the kingdom reeled from the attempts on their royal family. Had worked extensively with the security team, and although they hadn't discovered an inside man, their procedures had been sloppy, and the head of security had been happy to have Gideon as an advisor.

Then, they'd returned to the United States to the ranch. This time, with two of Alessandra's staff members as she worked on a proposal for a children's program that she'd been dreaming about for years. He'd had a few weeks to work with Nate and make some decisions about the ranch. Matt was back on active duty, and Gideon only had contact with him an occasional email and even rarer phone calls.

He and Alessandra had grown closer than ever. She'd been right that they could fit into each other's lives. He'd seen her nurturing spirit in the projects for which she chose to wield her influence. She made him laugh, made him notice the little things that he was often too busy to care about.

But there was still a part of him that worried things would fall apart. Something had happened between Carrie and Trey while he'd been in Glorvaird the first time, and although his sister had insisted that things were fine, he'd noticed the tension between them.

And while his feelings for Alessandra had deepened and grown...what if she wasn't ready for an engagement? What if she loved him, but she didn't want to marry him?

He knew there was protocol. That's why he was going to talk to her father first. But what if the man didn't approve? Gideon had no royal bloodlines. Although the ranch made a small profit most years, the real asset was their land. In no way was he considered rich.

Why in the world would the king agree?

But Gideon wasn't a coward, and he wasn't going to back down from this. He straightened the lapel of his suit jacket in the mirror and ran his comb through his hair once more—Alessandra had insisted he keep the beard—before gritting a frown and then turning for the door.

But before he left... He went to the suitcase once more and dug out the small, square jeweler's box he'd stowed beneath his drawers. For luck.

He'd had to work to convince the king's aide to give him the meeting, trusting the man with the real reason. Now he met the aide in the hall and followed the serious-faced fellow down another long hallway to a set of double-doors decorated with swirls of what might be real gold.

Gideon took one last deep breath as the doors swung open.

"You'll have a quarter hour," the assistant said in low tones as Gideon passed by him to enter the room.

The doors closed behind him.

The king sat behind a large cherry-wood desk ensconced in a fancy wheelchair. Alessandra had told Gideon what to expect when he eventually met her father—not knowing this was planned for today—but the man's wasted muscles and thinning white hair were still a shock. Gideon hid his reaction by bowing from the waist, the way he'd been instructed.

"Your Highness. Thank you for taking this meeting with me."

He straightened, meeting the King's stare. Though the man's body was failing him, there was no weakness in his shrewd gaze.

~ * ~

Alessandra sat across a small tea table from her older sister. Fine china and an elegant spread of pastries and fruit covered the white lacy tablecloth.

"So you're set on the American cowboy?"

Eloise wasn't one to mince words. Her sister's eyes met Alessandra's briefly and then skittered away. She didn't like to look at anyone in the face for very long. After years of being around her sister, Alessandra was used to it, though it still hurt.

Her sister's scars had never bothered Alessandra, not even when they'd been fresh and bright red, slashing across her cheek and neck, down into the shoulder of her blouses. But Eloise was incredibly sensitive about them.

She could also be incredibly rude.

"I love Gideon, yes," Alessandra answered.

Eloise picked apart the flaky pastry on her plate. "And I suppose you'll be spending a large amount of time in the States."

Alessandra frowned. She'd spoken to Eloise at-length after she'd arrived back in Glorvaird about her future plans. Eloise had agreed that she could cut back on some of her other events and take on some charity projects for children, ones that were close to her heart.

Was Eloise now thinking Alessandra would shirk her duties?

"We'll be spending some time at Gideon's home. His ranch has busy seasons where he's needed there."

Instead of acting upset, like Alessandra expected, Eloise nodded slowly. "Good. I have a project I need you to take on for me. It's very...sensitive."

Interest piqued, Alessandra leaned forward. "What kind of project?"

Eloise looked almost pained, if Alessandra had pegged her expression correctly. "This..." She shifted uncomfortably in her seat, and Alessandra had a moment of uncertainty. "Father recently confided in me that there was an infidelity when we were young."

Alessandra sat back in her seat, stunned. Of all the things she might've guessed, that wasn't one of them.

"There was a child. A daughter. Not legitimized, of course." Eloise looked down at the napkin in her lap. Alessandra still couldn't find words.

A sister. A half-sister.

"Her mother moved to America after the birth, and Father kept tabs on them for some time, but then the private investigator he'd hired lost them. Now, Father wants to find the girl. Before..."

Before he died. Alessandra's throat closed up. "I didn't think it was that close."

Eloise shrugged, her eyes on the window across. "The doctors say it might be as little as a year."

It wasn't nearly long enough. Being with Gideon had showed her that she could be brave enough to seek a deeper, reconciled relationship with her father, but... To only have such a limited time left brought a physical pain.

"Of course I'll help in whatever way I can," she said, a little hoarsely.

"I've two different investigators looking into finding her, but perhaps your man might have other contacts that would help."

Alessandra nodded. *Her man.* Yes, she'd enlist Gideon's help.

She wanted to get back to him now. To tell him of this new development. Talk through her muddled feelings about this revelation.

A sister.

~ * ~

When she found Gideon in the gardens, he seemed subdued. He glanced over his shoulder from where he stood near a stone bench in the rose arbor, and she saw his face was dark and brows were drawn. As she neared, she saw his suit jacket lying folded across one corner of the bench. And when he turned all the way around, she saw the tie he'd loosened around his neck.

She went to him and wrapped her arms around his waist. "What's the matter?"

She could feel the tension coiled in him, the tightness of his muscles.

"Nothing." His arms came around her upper back. He leaned back slightly, to better look into her face. "How was your sister?"

"Fine. I've got something to talk to you about." She squeezed his waist. "Later." And raised her face for his kiss.

He obliged her for a sweet kiss, but pulled away too soon.

"Something *is* the matter," she said with a slightly exaggerated moue. She reached up with one hand to touch his face, resting her palm against his cheek gently brushing with her thumb.

"No. I'm just...nervous."

"Nervous?" Her Gideon? Not likely. He broke their embrace and motioned for her to sit on the bench.

She humored him, perching on the edge of the cool stone. The scent of roses surrounded them and made the moment impossibly romantic. He stood tall, and she craned her neck to look up at him. One hand rested in his trouser pocket.

"I had everything planned perfectly for tonight, but...I don't think I can wait."

Then he dropped to one knee, and her stomach dipped. He reached for her with his empty hand, as his opposite hand brought a small black box out of his pocket. All her swirling thoughts stopped.

So did her breath.

"Alessandra, I love you. I can't imagine my life without you in it. Would you do me the honor of marrying me?"

She squeezed his hand tightly as tears blurred her vision. She blinked them back. "I love you, too. And...I'm so sorry to ruin your moment, but have you spoken to my father?"

One corner of his mouth tilted up. "Just this morning."

Her breathing eased. "And...? What did he say?"

"He gave his blessing."

She threw her arms around Gideon's neck, almost toppling them both. "Thank God."

She peppered his face with kisses until he took her

lips in a breath-stealing kiss. When they were both breathing hard, he pulled away and settled on the bench next to her.

"So that's a *yes*." It wasn't really a question, not the way he said it, slightly arrogant and more than a little relieved.

She leaned into his shoulder, watching as he pried open the black jeweler's box. "I would've married you anyway, without Father's blessing, but this makes it better..." Her thoughts, her words cut off as she caught sight of the ring. "Gideon..."

A large, sparkling diamond winked up at her, sunlight casting rainbows around it on Gideon's hands.

"It's too much." She didn't know the exact price tag, but a diamond like that must've cost his last two years' profits.

He cleared his throat. "I know we come from very different worlds, and I may never fit completely into yours, but I wanted to give you something fit for a princess."

He slipped it onto her finger, the metal cool against her skin. And because she was watching so closely, she noticed that his fingers were trembling.

She laced their fingers together, twisting the tangle of fingers to admire the darker tan of his skin against hers, and the sparkle of the ring.

"I love you," she said, looking into his dear face. "And *I'm* honored to be able to spend the rest of my life with you."

He steadied himself with a minute straightening of his shoulders, and she knew she'd said the right thing. Gideon might show the world a tough soldier, but she was the one who got to see the real man behind the facade.

That was the real treasure she valued. Gideon's heart.

COWBOY CHARMING

PROLOGUE

Fourteen-year-old Ethan Townsend stood next to his dad's hospital bed, shaking.

Terminal.

His thoughts circled like the wheels on his bike when he rode really fast. Wasn't a terminal part of the airport? Somewhere you went to check in for your flight? Not a diagnosis.

His dad was dying.

He nervously picked at the sheet that covered Dad's lower half. Dad reached out and clasped Ethan's hand.

How long had it been since Dad held his hand? His thoughts spun faster. The last time he could remember, he'd been ten, and his best friend had snubbed him in Cub Scouts.

Back then, Dad's hand was warm and rough, calloused from the work he did on the family-owned dairy farm.

Now Dad's skin was cool and clammy.

"I know it's hard, but I need you to be brave."

He couldn't look at his father, not yet. He stared through the half-open hospital-room door. His stepmother, Carol, stood in the hallway, sobbing silently into her hands.

How could Dad expect him to be brave? He was just a kid.

His jaw wobbled, and he clamped it tight, trying to keep the emotion he was bottling from spilling over.

"It's okay to cry, Ethan."

Dad tugged him closer, and he climbed into bed, curling up against his father the same way he had when he'd been five and they'd lost Mom.

"Don't ever let anyone tell you it's not okay to cry."

And he felt Dad's tears fall on his head.

Later, when they'd both cried themselves out, Dad let Ethan stay next to him in the bed.

"The dairy will provide for you and Carol and the boys. But with me gone, Robbie and Sam will need you to show them how to be real men."

He could barely think about his stepbrothers. Could barely think about the lessons Dad had taught him, usually when tossing a football around in the backyard.

Dad was supposed to be here to watch him start on the JV football team this fall.

He wasn't supposed to *die*.

Dad ruffled Ethan's hair when tears threatened again. "You've got your mother's courage." Dad's voice was rough, like he was close to tears, too. "Don't ever lose it."

~ * ~

Nineteen-year-old Ethan clutched the envelope in his hand, making the half-mile walk from the mailbox to the single-wide mobile home on the dairy farm. Two years ago, Carol had sold the house in town, and they'd been forced to move into this little trailer. He'd been born in that house. It held his memories of Mom and Dad.

Now, he slept on the living-room sofa while Robbie and Sam shared one of the two bedrooms. Carol had the other.

He'd been waiting for weeks for this envelope. It was going to be his ticket out of here.

The envelope was made from thick paper. Nice paper. *Embossed* with the university crest. And inside was his acceptance letter. He'd gotten in, even though he'd had to delay a year to help Carol make ends meet on the dairy.

She wasn't going to be happy he was leaving. But this was his chance to get the education he'd dreamed of since before his dad had died. He'd even been awarded a scholarship.

As he crested the slight rise leading up to the trailer and barn, shouts met his ears and drew his head up.

Eleven-year-old Robbie ran toward him, shouting. His expression was panic-stricken.

Ethan would've dismissed it as one of his stepbrothers' many pranks—always at his expense—except for the tears streaming down Robbie's face.

"It's Mom!"

Two hours later, Ethan sat in the hospital waiting

room between his stepbrothers. The same numbness he'd felt after his dad's death had stolen over him, though to a lesser degree. He hadn't loved Carol. She'd given him a roof over his head and—most of the time—three meals a day. But she'd also expected a lot of him. He'd been running the dairy since he was sixteen. He'd never gotten to play JV football, or varsity. When he wasn't working the dairy, she'd expected him to maintain the trailer and the yard— though Robbie was old enough now to run the push mower.

Before he'd turned sixteen, she'd fired two managers, run up her credit card bills, and lost so much revenue that she'd been forced to sell off most of the land and a number of the producing cows. Which meant that no matter what he did, they barely eked out a living. If they ever had extra, she spent it on new clothes for her and the boys.

Ethan wore secondhand clothes from the Goodwill store. Just as well, since he was usually up to his knees in muck.

College was supposed to be his ticket out, but the doctor had just delivered the worst news possible.

Carol was gone.

The boys had no other relatives.

Which meant there was no one else to look after them. *He* was their closest relative.

Looking down at them now, Robbie at eleven, and Sam at ten, Ethan remembered what it had felt like when Dad died. How could he abandon them to the system?

He couldn't.

CHAPTER ONE

Six years later

Princess Mia, third in line for the crown of Glorvaird, stood in the shade of a big, red Texas barn and watched a real cattle operation.

The October sun warmed everything, baking the brown grasses in the fields and the cowboys working there. But the wind carried a distinct chill that had her shivering in her jean jacket. She was used to mild, rainy weather in the coastal kingdom of Glorvaird, but this dry wind was new and made her nose itch.

She'd traveled to the States a few times before on royal business, but always to one of the bigger cities. New York. L.A. This was her first experience with country life.

So far she had to admit the view wasn't bad. Cowboys prowled everywhere, all of them busy bringing a long line of cows through a series of pens and then chutes where a cowboy shoved some kind of tube into the cow's mouth and medication was dispensed down their throat.

It was disgusting work.

Her sister, Princess Alessandra, sat atop a rail

fence, avidly watching. It was smelly, loud work as the cattle bawled and milled, stirring up dust. She couldn't imagine what her sister found so fascinating.

Or maybe she could. Alessandra was likely watching the love of her life, ranch owner Gideon Hale, who worked amid the other cowboys. The sunlight sparkled off the diamond ring she wore on her left hand.

Mia was only a little jealous.

She was aware of the admiring glances she kept receiving from the men as they moved around the yard. Gideon and Alessandra had introduced her to a few of the hands, but there were several others whom she hadn't met yet.

Texas had its fair share of handsome cowboys.

And all of them seemed to enjoy looking at her.

Except one.

The auburn-haired cowboy—at least what she could see of his hair beneath the tan cowboy hat he wore—hadn't glanced at her once.

It shouldn't bother her. She shouldn't be curious about him. It wasn't that he was withdrawn, because he spoke several times to the men he was working with, and she saw him smile more than once. It was that he was the only man on the place, other than Gideon, who hadn't looked at her once.

And so what if she was used to attention, admiring glances? She couldn't forget the promise she'd made herself back in Glorvaird. She wasn't going to kiss another man until she was sure he was the one she'd marry.

Which meant she really shouldn't even be looking at the cowboy. At any cowboy.

She was only twenty-three and had five failed relationships behind her. One for each year since her eighteenth birthday.

Was she so wrong to long for true love?

She was glad to have been included in this trip with Alessandra and Gideon. Her sister had asked for her help with final preparations for the big engagement ball that she and Gideon were throwing in three weeks. There would be a similar ball in Glorvaird, but Alessandra wanted this party to celebrate with their American friends, for whom it wouldn't be cost effective to travel so far for a party, though some would come to the royal wedding in her home country.

And Mia had wanted to get away from the media storm still raging after her last, very public, breakup.

She'd thought being here would be a distraction.

She just hadn't planned on the distraction being a handsome cowboy who refused to look in her direction.

~ * ~

Ethan couldn't help but be aware of the beautiful blonde.

He'd first noticed her mid-morning, when she and another blonde had emerged from the ranch house to watch the chaos ensuing near the barn.

Their appearances were similar enough that he

thought they must be sisters, though he didn't know either of them. The blonde, who he guessed was the older sister, wore jeans and a man's work coat. Her boots had seen their fair share of farm work. He guessed the coat must belong to Gideon because at one point, she'd stopped him, and they'd shared a warm kiss.

But the younger sister... she wore skinny jeans that hugged her slender curves, and a white blouse beneath a rhinestone-studded denim jacket.

Nobody who worked on a ranch wore white around farm chores. And her high-heeled boots were more appropriate for a fashion event than the barnyard.

Regardless, he couldn't keep from sneaking glances at her. At first, she hung back, perching on an ice chest closer to the barn than the corrals where they ran cows through.

But soon enough, she was moving among the guys, distributing cold bottles of water out of the ice chest. She made it a point to speak to the different hands.

The October weather couldn't be called brisk, and the work was grueling. He'd sweated through the T-shirt he wore beneath a flannel overshirt. The sweat was downright refreshing compared to the cow drool and medication that had been slung onto him by the ornery beasts. He was sure he smelled worse than the bovines they were drenching with worming medication.

Finally, it was his turn to take a break from the

drenching position—sticking the elongated tube down the cows' throats and squeezing de-worming medication down their gullets.

He'd take five and then climb back in and start driving cows into the chute. Another hour and a half, and he could take a short break in the AC in his truck before heading home to start the afternoon milking. Taking on this extra job would make for a couple of eighteen hour days, but the extra cash was needed at home. Like always. His stepbrothers were demanding new kicks.

He leaned on the railing, not holding his breath for the beautiful young woman to head his way with one of those water bottles.

He'd learned early on that girls like her never gave the time of day to guys like him. He hadn't seen her around town before, and there was no doubt she was related to the beautiful blonde that was Gideon Hale's girlfriend, but somehow he knew that she'd know just by looking at him that he was hired help. Dirt poor hired help.

"Thirsty?"

The lilting female voice shocked him into looking up before he'd thought better of it. She was right there, extending a bottle still dripping from the ice water in the chest.

He pushed his hat back slightly on his head and took it. "Thank you, ma'am. Miss."

His face went hot as he stumbled—didn't younger women hate to be called ma'am?—and he cursed his fair coloring, knowing he was probably blushing.

She was even more beautiful up close, with dancing, ice-blue eyes and the lightest splash of freckles across her nose and high cheekbones. Her long, blonde hair was pulled behind her head in a curly ponytail.

"You can call me Mia." Her smile had him noticing her shapely lips. "No, 'miss' required."

He swallowed hard. "I'm Ethan Townsend."

Her flowery, feminine scent was noticeable, probably because he stank so badly. That realization just made him blush harder.

He expected her to walk away, having done the polite thing by not leaving him out as she was handing out cold drinks. To his surprise, she propped her pretty, pointy-toed boot on the bottom railing and leaned her elbows on the fence next to him.

"So, Ethan. How long have you worked on the Triple H?"

He'd taken a gulp of the cold water, and now swallowed it wrong. It burned all the way down. He cleared his throat.

"I'm just extra help for a couple of days."

"Oh, I didn't realize."

There was a short, awkward pause, and then she asked, "What do you do?"

"I run a dairy farm on the opposite side of town." He didn't like to say he owned the farm, because really, the bank owned it. Carol had mortgaged it to the hilt, and he was lucky to make the payments and keep enough cash for himself and the boys to eat. Teenaged boys weren't cheap to feed.

"That must be a fun job."

Fun. Said the woman who'd obviously never had to be on the clock at four a.m. She'd probably never even thought about cleaning machinery and shoveling cow patties until your eyes crossed, and then doing it all over again in the afternoon.

And repeating it. Every single day.

He didn't nod, couldn't lie, though he softened it with what smile he could dredge up. "It's something." Hopefully only for another three years, but he couldn't focus too hard on that. Couldn't afford to jinx himself.

He was no expert in holding his own in a conversation with a beautiful woman, but it seemed like it was his turn to say something. "Are you just visiting our part of Texas?"

She tilted her head to one side, her brows furrowed slightly in a way that shouldn't be so adorable. Like she couldn't figure him out. She glanced over to where Gideon's girlfriend sat and then back to him. "Yes, for a few weeks."

And then Brian, one of the Triple H hands, rode by inside the temp fence they'd constructed early that morning, his horse kicking up dust. "Townsend, you about done flirting with the princess? I know it's a treat having a real royal highness around, but you ain't getting paid to stand there."

He was used to the ribbing from the Triple H hands. They were a tight-knit group, and when he got hired on for the most unpleasant tasks, like today's drenching and springtime steer cutting, they made him a part of the pack.

But this joke hit him right in the solar plexus. Princess? This gal was a princess?

Brian laughed. "You didn't know? How could you not know, man?"

Most days, he barely had time to eat. His stepbrothers had the only TV in the house in their bedroom, and they couldn't afford to take the paper.

And ever since last summer, he'd blocked his ears from all town gossip.

He could barely glance at her, but when he did, he noticed the color high on her cheeks. "I think it's refreshing," she called out to Brian, who was already spreading Ethan's humiliation to the next closest cowhand.

She slid a glance to him, offered a smile. "My sister is engaged to Gideon."

There must be a story there, but his throat had closed up. He wouldn't have asked anyway.

He'd been standing here next to a real, live princess and probably making himself look a fool. As if he needed any help with that.

He'd grabbed the water and now forced it down his gullet, twisting the cap back on the empty bottle. He tossed it in a nearby barrel and nodded at the beautiful princess who'd given him the time of day. "Thank you."

He didn't dare glance at her as he ducked through the railing and back into the corral.

He was such a dunce.

~ * ~

Alessandra rubbed her eye sockets, blinking away the after-glare from staring at her laptop screen for too long. She was curled up on the couch in Gideon's living room, only one lamp lighting the space. Gideon's German Shepherd Dog Apollo snored softly from his cushion near the front door.

Though she was frustrated with her self-assigned task, she was glad to be on the Triple H. It felt like home, maybe more so than her suite of rooms at the castle in Glorvaird. Her kingdom was part bustling metropolis and part seaside village, but when she was there, she missed the wide-open spaces of Gideon's north Texas ranch.

"You still up?"

Gideon stood in the doorway, leaning one broad shoulder against the jamb. He'd told her he needed to work on the ranch's books for a while, but that had been... she checked the clock on her laptop's screen. Nearly three hours ago. He'd untucked his shirt and now stood in sock feet, apparently ready to go to bed.

"I thought this would be easier," she admitted, closing the laptop's screen and pushing it away on the couch cushion. Before she'd left Glorvaird, her older sister Eloise had delivered a piece of unexpected news—that the princesses had a half-sister from an affair their father'd had years ago—and tasked Alessandra with finding the lost princess.

Gideon came closer, and Alessandra stood, stretching her stiff muscles. She'd been so zoned-in to her search on the computer, following rabbit trail after rabbit trail.

Gideon's hands closed over her elbows, sliding slowly up her arms as he held her close.

"It'll take time," he said into her hair.

She knew he'd put out feelers with his contacts in the military—Gideon was a former Navy SEAL. She also knew her older sister had hired two private investigators to try and find the girl—woman now—who'd fallen off the map several years ago.

Her father wanted to see his long-lost daughter before he died. And though the doctor could only estimate when that might be, the clock was ticking. Alessandra felt the unknown deadline pressing down on her, and with it, a desire to return to Glorvaird to try and build the closer relationship with her father that she'd always wanted.

If Father was willing. When he'd first been diagnosed with MS, he hadn't wanted to make any changes to his lifestyle, hadn't wanted to spend more time with his daughters, even though his time on earth was limited.

That still hurt, but she was determined not to let her father go without fighting for a closer relationship.

Now that loving Gideon had shown her what a real relationship, built from true love, could look like.

Just being close to her fiancé like this made her frustration start to fall away. She leaned her head against his shoulder. His hands moved up even more, rubbing gentle circles into her shoulders and the back of her neck, loosening muscles gone tight from inactivity.

"You tell Mia yet?"

"No." As Gideon would say, that was the other burr under her saddle. Eloise had told Alessandra about their lost sister, and it had been a total shock. Eloise hadn't told Mia. She'd left it up to Alessandra when to break the news.

Alessandra was still coming to terms with it herself. Her mother had died when she was small, just five years old. Mia had been even smaller at three. She had no memories of their mother. If Alessandra had felt betrayed at hearing this news about their father, what would Mia feel? Father had been the only parent she'd known.

Plus, she was still trying to navigate the changing relationship with her younger sister. It wasn't until Alessandra's life had been threatened by an assassination attempt that she'd faced the reality of how broken their family had become. With Father caught up in his royal duties and now pushing many of those duties onto the crown princess, there was no real family structure.

And Alessandra wanted a real family. When she'd come to Gideon's ranch, lost and alone, she'd found the family she'd been looking for. And she wanted to rebuild what could be with her own family.

If Mia found out she'd been keeping this secret—for over two weeks now—she'd be hurt. It might put a wedge between the tentative friendship they'd been expanding since Alessandra had returned to Glorvaird after the assassination attempt.

Gideon's magic fingers relaxed her so much that her head fell back.

Which must've been what he wanted, because it gave him access to her face. His calloused hands moved to cup her jaw, and he lowered his mouth to hers, kissing her with a gentle intensity that had her tingling all the way down to her toes.

Her hands rested on his muscled chest, amazed at the power harnessed there, amazed that this virile, powerful man loved her back.

He pressed kisses against her temple and cheek, finally pressing his jaw to her ear.

Her racing heart still hadn't slowed.

"What about you?" she asked. "Did you get your books balanced?" She didn't know anything about the ranch's accounting, but Gideon carried a heavy load with managing the ranch, which his stepfather had left to the three Hales, Gideon, his brother Matt, and his sister Carrie. When Gideon had declared his love for Alessandra, he'd also given up some of the rigid control, leaving more of running the ranch in the foreman's hands. The ranch also employed four other hands to care for the large spread and keep it running smoothly.

It wasn't easy for Gideon to be away for long periods of time. But he'd done it because he loved her.

Now she felt the tension coiled in him. She realized he hadn't answered her question. "What?" she whispered.

"Something's going on," he said. "There's a

discrepancy in the accounting. I haven't found what it is yet, but it wasn't there before we left for Glorvaird."

Her stomach pitched. "What does that mean? Someone's stealing from the Triple H?"

He shrugged slightly, his chest moving beneath her hands. "I don't know yet. It could be an honest mistake." She knew Gideon though, knew he'd seen some of the worst things human beings could do to each other during his missions. He had to be suspicious that it wasn't a mistake. "If one of the hands is responsible, I don't want them to know I've figured anything out yet. Can you keep this is a secret?"

"Of course." She stretched up slightly on her toes and pressed a kiss against his bearded cheek.

"If I'm tied up with this, I'll have to take some time away from the details of the engagement party."

She loved that he called it a party when it was really a full-fledged ball.

"That's all right. I've got Mia here to help, and the event coordinator has handled most of the details." The time they split between Glorvaird and Texas necessitated that they utilized one of the premiere party planners in Dallas. "Since we've already found the venue, it's more about coordinating with the florist and decorators. And finding my dress."

"And managing the security team," he reminded her. "I'll make time for that."

She couldn't help smiling. "And the security team." Since her near-assassination, Gideon had been overprotective. Not that she minded having him close, and protecting was in his nature.

But how would his protective nature react if he discovered someone was stealing from the Triple H?

CHAPTER TWO

Ethan was elbow-deep scrubbing dog poop out of the kennels when he was paged to the front of the veterinarian's office.

In addition to the odd jobs he picked up, he worked three days a week as a kennel assistant. Mostly cleaning cages. Sometimes clipping a dog's or cat's nails or exercising the dogs who were boarding.

And occasionally, if there was a difficult animal, usually a large dog, the vet would ask for his help when the technicians—most of them vets in training—needed it.

Turned out, he was good with difficult animals.

Just not difficult brothers.

Without the education he'd given up his one shot at, this work was the closest he could get to his dream job.

He joined the vet, Suzanne, and the tech in the larger of the two exam rooms, surprised into hesitating in the doorway when he caught sight of the blonde head bent over a good-sized German Shepherd Dog he recognized. The animal must be edging close to eighty pounds, all muscle.

It wasn't the dog that had his stomach clenching. It was the woman holding its leash.

She looked up, her hair falling in a golden cascade over her shoulder. His initial guess had been correct. It *was* the princess. Mia.

He hadn't been able to stop thinking about her in the three days since he'd seen her at the Triple H. Today she wore slim slacks with dressy flat shoes and a fuzzy pale green sweater.

Movement caught his eye, and he remembered there were others in the room. Suzanne stood beside the exam table but hadn't approached the dog yet. The usual tech, Candy, was at the vet's elbow, also not approaching the dog.

"Good old Apollo," he said because he didn't know whether it was appropriate to say hello to a princess, or even if he should.

He smelled like dog poop and probably looked like it too. Not that it mattered when Mia was so far out of his realm.

Her expression eased into a smile. "Hi, Ethan."

She remembered his name.

And he didn't miss the vet's sideways look.

"This guy giving you ladies trouble?" He stepped right up to the dog, pushing away the hesitancy he'd felt moments ago. He had to provide a steady presence for the dog, so it would calm down and endure the exam. "I'm a little surprised one of the guys didn't bring him in."

"Trey is outside," Mia explained. "I caught a ride to town with him and Apollo, but he had to take an important phone call." Mia surrendered the leash to Ethan, and their fingers brushed. He worked at schooling his face into a neutral expression, not wanting to show the *zing* that'd traveled up his arm and straight to his gut.

Candy ducked out of the room, apparently content to let Ethan handle the dog. He'd seen Apollo for the last two annual exams. The big guy did not appreciate the rectal thermometer or the needles that delivered his shots.

Mia stepped back, and Ethan ran his hands down the dog's back and shoulders. Apollo's ears relaxed a little, and Ethan nodded to the vet, who approached with a confident gait.

"Ethan is our resident dog whisperer," Suzanne said, and he felt Mia's curious gaze on him. He kept his focus on the dog.

"He can calm down any unruly animal," the vet continued. "Even this guy."

He was aware of Mia slightly behind him and at his elbow but kept his face angled toward the dog. Maybe she wouldn't see him blushing this time.

"Apollo isn't so bad," he said, with a scratch of the dog's chest. He kept his hand there while the vet manipulated the dog's back legs and feet, checking his joints and muscle movement.

"Is this another of your odd jobs?" Mia asked curiously.

Suzanne answered before he could. "Ethan started volunteering here when he was ten. We had high hopes that he'd join the practice."

The vet moved to Apollo's head, and Ethan moved back a bit, allowing her the room she needed to check the dog's teeth, eyes, and ears.

Suzanne couldn't know how much of a blow her words were, casual as they were spoken. He'd wanted it too, so very badly.

"You know there's still scholarship money earmarked with your name," Suzanne said.

Okay, maybe she did know.

She brought it up every few months, as if he could ever forget it. What did she hope to accomplish now, bringing it up in front of the princess?

He'd tried to keep up with his education that first year after Carol passed. Enrolled in six hours of online classes. It had been impossible to keep up while caring for a ten- and eleven-year-old and running the dairy.

He smiled stiffly at Suzanne, who went on with the exam as if she'd been talking about the weather, not his life. She engaged the princess in conversation about her impressions of Texas.

At four years old, Apollo was in the prime of his life, and it didn't take much longer to give him his vaccinations.

Ethan's heart rate came down after the princess had left the room. The vet was paged for an urgent phone call, and he found himself alone in the exam room. He took out the industrial-strength cleaner beneath the cabinets and wiped down the floor where Apollo had stood for his examination, then disposed of the needles properly.

He was on his way back to the kennels when the front desk paged him to take a phone call. He ducked into the small employee lunch room, heart pounding. In his experience, surprise phone calls were usually bad news.

He was right.

The high school office asked him to come down. He had just enough time before the afternoon milking.

He met his stepbrothers in the hallway just outside the principal's office. They sat on hard plastic chairs, both wearing sullen expressions.

"It wasn't our fault," Sam muttered.

It never was.

No matter what he said or did, the boys seemed to have a problem with authority. Unlike his dad with him, Carol hadn't instilled any respect in them at all.

Maybe it was because she hadn't respected Ethan, no matter what he'd done for the family, what he'd sacrificed.

Things had come to a head last winter, when his brothers had been picked up by the sheriff's office for defacing one of the buildings on Main Street with spray paint. And the half-empty twelve-pack of beer cans they'd been caught with hadn't won them any brownie points. The business owner had pressed charges, and Robbie and Sam had had to go in front of the county judge. They'd been sentenced to forty hours of community service each.

Ethan had hoped the event had scared them straight, and it had, for a few months.

But then, the boys' behavior had become increasingly worse. He'd had two calls from their teachers in the past month.

The principal, a woman in her mid-fifties with slate-gray hair, stuck her head out the office door. "Coach wants you boys at football practice. I'd like to see you again in the morning, before your first class."

Robbie rolled his eyes.

Ethan nudged his foot, and both boys heaved aggravated sighs.

"Fine," Robbie muttered.

They scooted down the hall toward the locker rooms, leaving Ethan to enter the principal's office alone.

He'd never visited when he'd been in high school.

She steepled her fingers on the edge of her desk after they'd both sat down. "There's been another incident."

He took the chair across from her, praying he wasn't getting anything nasty on the upholstery. "I'm sorry."

It was his standard answer. They both knew it. They both knew he *was* sorry. He just didn't know how to make his stepbrothers feel regret.

Somehow, Carol had made them believe they could get away with whatever they wanted. No matter how many times he grounded them or took away their video games, they couldn't seem to understand that their actions had consequences.

In two more years, Robbie had a chance to get out of this town. To go to college and *be* something.

"Both boys were in Sam's classroom before the bell rang and were cutting up with some friends. The teacher overheard some inappropriate things and asked the boys to quit the conversation. But Robbie and Sam shouted at the teacher. They cursed at him and were threatening bodily harm before another teacher and myself diffused the situation. They've both received detentions after football practice for a week."

Ethan nodded, stunned. How could his stepbrothers do something like this?

"There's another issue that we need to discuss. Both your stepbrothers are failing their French classes. If they can't get their grades up by mid-term, they won't be eligible to finish the football season."

Now Ethan felt as if he'd been sucker-punched. "How bad is it? Is there make up work they can do?"

"I've talked to the French teacher, and unless they put some real work into it, they're going to be so far behind that they'll never catch up. He's offered two make-up tests. *Verbal* tests."

She reached a piece of paper over the desk, and he took it with a sense of doom. He knew the boys had to have two foreign-language credits to get into college. Sam was enrolled in the basic-level French, while Robbie was taking his second year. And that with their mediocre grades, football scholarships were the only way they were going to be able to afford tuition.

He stared at the paper in his hand. He'd barely passed his own high school foreign language classes because he'd been working so many hours outside of school. And that had been years ago. There was no way could he tutor them himself. And with their budget so tight, how could he afford to pay someone?

The principal sighed. She stood and came around the desk, leaning her hip against its edge.

"Ethan." She sighed, and he braced himself.

"Have you thought about just... letting the boys go?"

That was totally unexpected.

Letting them go?

"Everyone in town admired what you did when your stepmother died. God knows you didn't have to take on the care of two minors when you were that young."

At the time, he hadn't felt as if he'd had a choice. The boys had needed him, and he'd had those memories of his father's death burned into his mind.

"You've nearly killed yourself since you were sixteen to keep that farm going, and none of your family appreciated you. Robbie and Sam are old enough now to understand consequences. I don't think anybody would blame you if you let them go into the system."

He couldn't find words. His gut reaction was denial. How could he turn his back on his stepbrothers? When they'd lost so much, just like he had. He was the only family they had left.

He shoved to his feet, the turmoil in his gut causing enough agitation that he couldn't remain seated. "Thanks for your concern. I'll talk to them about—" He waved the paper still clutched in his hand.

"Ethan."

He was enough of a rule-follower that he stopped in the doorway.

"I didn't mean to cause offense." Her voice and expression conveyed apology, but he wasn't offended. Just shocked.

"You've given so much...first to your stepmother, and now to the boys. But what about yourself? When do you get to live?"

Heat burned his face. He didn't have an answer. If he didn't work the dairy, they didn't eat. Just making their bills left him no time for anything else—much less figuring out a plan.

He excused himself, making his way out of the quiet school while the principal's words clattered in his mind.

The visitors' lot was adjacent to the football field, and he stopped near the chain-link fence that separated the field from the sidewalk. He rested his palm on the cool metal bar at the top of the fence.

Let them go? All the years he'd cared for his brothers, he'd never considered sending them into the system. Foster care.

It felt horrible to think it, but the idea was appealing. They'd never appreciated all he'd done for them, no more than their mother had. He could relinquish his ornery stepbrothers to the state and get on with his life.

But they were family—sort of. Hadn't he promised his father he'd show them how to be real men? He hadn't done that yet. And even though they were more trouble than a stall full of cow dung, they were his brothers.

Stepbrothers who, at the rate they were going, wouldn't make it into college, scholarship or not. He'd staked everything, his entire future, on the fact that the boys would leave for college after graduation.

Today's news was especially painful after the vet's reminder of what he'd given up.

One of the coaches shouted, and the offensive line, including Robbie and Sam, rushed forward, smashing their bodies against a series of weighted sleds with dummies atop them. Ethan's brothers rammed into those dummies like they rammed through life, destroying everything in their path without as much as a glance to see the damage they left in their wake.

What was he supposed to do if they lost their chance to go to college? He wouldn't continue to support them past their eighteenth birthdays. College was their chance to make something of themselves. A chance he hadn't had.

How could he convince them not to squander it?

From further down the field, the quarterback threw a long, spiral pass to one of the receivers under the watchful eyes of the assistant coach.

Ethan would have given anything to have played. He'd started on peewee teams at five. He and his dad had loved playing catch. Making plans for JV and varsity. If his dad had lived, Ethan knew he would've been at every game. They'd even talked a little about what colleges Ethan might go to on a football scholarship, when it was time.

But all those dreams had died with Dad.

This was Ethan's reality now. He needed to find a way to convince Robbie and Sam to straighten up for these last two years of school. To move on. Then, when they were both gone, he could start making plans for himself.

~ * ~

Trey's mysterious phone call had led to a mysterious errand, which left Mia and Apollo at loose ends.

Today's crisp autumn weather was lovely, and she didn't mind taking the dog for a walk, though she was aware of the two royal security team members following not far behind. She was more aware of them than ever, after the limousine she'd been riding in had nearly been the victim of a bombing a few months ago in Glorvaird.

Apollo had relaxed since his exam, since they'd left the veterinarian's office. Now he walked jauntily at her side.

She'd turned off of quaint Main Street and onto a more residential road, and before she knew it, they'd stumbled upon the local high school.

Curious, mostly because she'd never had any typical high school experiences, only tutors, she let herself and Apollo wander in that direction.

She was rounding a lush, green exercise field of some sort when she caught sight of a familiar figure, standing alone at the fence.

Ethan.

Perhaps it was her day to run into the cowboy-farmer-jack-of-all-trades. He'd been professional and polite in the vet's office earlier. No sign of the blushing young man that had ducked his head shyly at the Triple H. She didn't know why, but she was surprised to have discovered that at one time he'd had bigger dreams.

What had stopped him from chasing them?

Now he appeared pensive. Maybe upset. What was he doing at the school anyway? He was too young to have high school-aged children.

She should leave it alone. Leave him alone, but she found her feet carrying her in that direction anyway.

She hadn't been paying attention to the activity on the field beyond the cowboy, but as she moved to join him, several young men wearing padding and helmets crashed into each other, tackling one another to the ground.

She jumped, Apollo lunged, and she squeaked as she gripped his leash tighter. Ethan turned toward her.

She didn't know what expression he wore, if he were surprised to see here, because she couldn't tear her eyes from the players who were... it looked like they were lining up to get ready to tackle each other again!

The hand that wasn't holding Apollo's leash came up to cover her mouth.

"I guess you've never seen American football before," Ethan said dryly, finally pulling her gaze to him.

He'd lost the pensive look he'd worn before he'd known she was there, but instead of smiling, he wore a slightly-guarded look. Or maybe haunted.

Whatever it was, it bothered her.

She didn't know him from Adam, but from that first day, there'd been something that drew her to him. And while she knew she couldn't make everyone happy, she could usually draw a smile from most people.

"This would be my first taste of American football," she agreed, stepping slightly closer.

Ethan bent to greet Apollo, and the dog gave him a happy smile and a wag of his tail, not holding against Ethan what had happened in the vet's office earlier.

"They're practicing...?" she guessed of the football players.

"Yeah." He scratched Apollo's ears and straightened to his full height, his Stetson throwing shadows across his face. "Not as much now that season is here, but twice a day in the early fall."

Something in his expression... a wistfulness as he watched the players, prompted her to ask, "Did you play?"

Now a shadow passed behind his eyes. "No."

He didn't offer more of an explanation, but somehow she knew there was something he wasn't saying.

He nodded to the field. "My stepbrothers are out there. Robbie and Sam."

She looked but couldn't differentiate one boy from another with their identical, unnumbered training jerseys and helmets.

"So they just...keep crashing into each other?" she asked.

She wasn't looking directly at him but had enough of a view of his face to see the side of his mouth quirk up. "No. In a real game, the goal is to get the ball into the other team's end zone. That's the other end of the field. It's how you score points."

"And the other team wants to stop you?" she asked. "Thus, the...crashing?"

"Tackling. Yeah, you've got it." He had a nice smile, when he'd relaxed enough to show it. "Football is pretty intense around here. The whole town gets into it. You should take in a game while you're in town."

"Oh, that'd be fun! When?"

She watched in fascination as his face filled with color in a wave from his chin to the place where his forehead disappeared into his hat. He coughed a little into his fist.

"Erm, there's a game on Friday night." His voice sounded a little as if he'd swallowed a frog.

"Lovely! You could pick me up. What time should I be ready?"

His face had gone an even deeper shade of red, and she wondered if he'd spend the whole of Friday night looking as if he'd choked something down the wrong pipe.

"Six, I guess."

One of her security team cleared his throat, and she looked behind to see him jerking his chin, like they needed to be going. She sighed and turned back to the cowboy. "Here, let me borrow your phone."

He looked flummoxed, and she couldn't help the smile that pulled at her lips. "I'll input my number, in case you need to reach me."

He dug in his front pocket and came up with an older model flip-phone. She schooled her reaction, because she hadn't seen one in years. Tilted her head. "You know what, why don't you add your number to mine?"

She drew her metallic, thin smart phone, from her pocket, and with a few flicks of her fingers, pulled up her contacts list.

He fumbled it when she handed him the phone. "Sorry," he muttered.

She couldn't help noticing his calloused hands as he input the digits and wondered what it would feel like to have one of them holding hers. Of all the men she'd dated—royals and businessmen and the one soccer player—none of them had been anything like Ethan.

Maybe that was why she was so drawn to him.

She pondered it as she took her phone back, said a quick goodbye, and turned her steps back toward the street where Trey had parked the Triple H's farm truck. She couldn't help looking over her shoulder as she walked away.

Ethan had returned to leaning on the fence, his posture once again slightly withdrawn.

She had to remember her promise. No matter how much she was attracted to the shy cowboy, she wasn't kissing *anyone*. Not until she met *the* one.

But that didn't mean she couldn't enjoy the company of one handsome cowboy.

CHAPTER THREE

Ethan wasn't sure exactly how this had happened as he turned his truck down the Triple H's drive just after six on Friday night.

Somehow, he'd been wrangled into a date with Princess Mia.

Him.

On a date.

With a princess.

He'd cleaned out most of the junk that regularly accumulated in his truck, but he'd hoped to have time to run it through the car wash and vacuum it. Unfortunately, an issue with one of the milking machines had delayed him by an hour this afternoon, and he'd barely gotten a shower.

So he'd stuck one of those air fresheners on the heating vent and hoped for the best.

There wasn't any use in pretending to be something he wasn't. His truck was fifteen years old, the same one that Dad had bought for the dairy before he'd passed.

If she hadn't already figured out that Ethan wasn't made of money, she would soon.

Surprisingly, they'd texted a couple of times since Wednesday. The first time her name had popped up his phone's screen, he'd stared for a good minute before he'd decided to answer.

Mia: what does one wear to a high school football game?

He was twenty-six and had never dated before. No one that he'd been interested in had been interested in him, for obvious reasons.

He'd fumbled his way through a response.

Ethan: jeans.
Mia: I won't be out of place without a team sweatshirt or something?
Ethan: No.

The next day, she'd texted him mid-morning, but when he'd expected another query about the football game, instead she'd asked whether he could teach her to ride a horse. When he'd agreed, she'd sent:

Mia: Good, then we need to schedule date #2.

He'd stared at that one for even longer than her first, unexpected message. *Date #2?* That meant she thought of the football game as Date #1, didn't it?

No idea what to do with that.

So here he was, a moron who didn't know quite what to expect going on a date with someone so out of his stratosphere. Out of his galaxy, even.

One at a time, he rubbed his sweaty hands on his jeans.

He pulled into the Triple H drive, as always, unable to keep from enjoying the rolling pastures as the old truck slowly rolled toward the house. Being here always reminded him of what he'd lost with Dad's passing. Land. Home. Security.

When he reached the ranch house, two guys in dark suits and even darker glasses strode off the porch. They met him as he got out of the truck. While he hadn't known Mia was a princess that very first day, he'd certainly gotten a crash course. This must be her security team.

"You got anything on you? Weapons, drugs?" One of the guys asked the questions as the other one cranked open the truck door and leaned inside. Without permission.

"No," Ethan said.

Apparently they weren't taking his word for it. The guy forcibly turned Ethan around and started patting him down. Ethan wore a long-sleeved T-shirt beneath his corduroy jacket and jeans. There wasn't any place to hide anything interesting, and the security guy was done in moments.

It didn't stop Ethan from being embarrassed as the goon backed off, leaving Ethan to turn and face the house.

"Gideon!" He thought that was Mia's voice calling out from inside, though it might've been her sister.

What had he gotten himself into? He left the security guys to search his truck and headed for the house. When he hit the porch steps, he could see inside the half-open front door. Mia had her hands on her hips and was staring down the rancher, though she was a head shorter. "You promised your goons wouldn't harass Ethan."

That she'd used the same word to describe them as Ethan had cheered him.

"Just because we're in Texas, and just because Ethan's done some jobs for me, doesn't mean I can forgo basic safety precautions. There's still a real threat against the Glorvaird crown and I have to—"

"Is there *really*?" she demanded, and he had to admire the fire blazing from her eyes. He was a little glad it wasn't directed at him. "Because *nothing has happened* in months."

"That doesn't mean that nothing will happen," Gideon returned.

She hesitated, her shoulders heaving with breath as if she'd been about to blast him again.

"Um, knock knock?" Ethan said through the open door.

Mia turned to him immediately, her blonde hair billowing in a curtain behind her. He got a look at the slim black pants and that rhinestone-encrusted jean jacket she'd worn the day they'd met. She looked relieved to have an out from the conversation with her soon-to-be brother-in-law.

She motioned him in, and he stepped over the threshold.

"I'm really sorry," she said quietly, looking up into his eyes with a sincerity that couldn't be faked.

He got tongue-tied in the face of her beauty and had to settle for a shrug. "It's okay," he finally managed.

She looked over his shoulder, frowning, and he followed her gaze to see the security guys sweeping beneath his truck with a mirror on a stick. Were they seriously looking for a bomb or something?

He shook his head slightly. "They won't find anything."

"Good." Gideon moved forward and clapped Ethan on the shoulder. "What time you do expect to have her back?"

"All right, Dad," Mia said with an exaggerated elbow to Gideon's gut, edging him back and out of the conversation. "I'm not a teenager, and I'll be back when I feel like it."

Gideon frowned, but Mia didn't wait for him to say anything else. She slipped her hand into Ethan's and tugged him toward the door.

The shock of having her soft, slender fingers wrapped in his rendered him speechless.

"I'm really sorry," she said again. "Alessandra says Gideon's been overreacting ever since someone targeted her... She nearly died."

She had?

When they reached his truck, the two security guys moved off. Instead of going around to the passenger side, like he expected, she yanked open the driver's side door and climbed inside, sliding across the bench seat.

He followed her in.

She took a breath, looking out the window. "There was also a bomb, back in Glorvaird. I was in a limo, and the bomb exploded pretty close to where we were driving past. Shattered my window."

She glanced back at him, tried for a smile, but he saw the shadows in her eyes. "Things have been quiet ever since."

"That must've been scary," he said slowly. "I guess I can understand why Gideon's so protective."

Her smile turned a little wry. "Good. Because we'll have an escort."

He cranked the engine and then followed her gaze to the black sedan that was edging out from beside the ranch house. So her security would come with them.

How frightening must it have been to live through that? He could deal with the security if it kept Mia safe.

She seemed to breathe easier as they turned out of the ranch drive and onto the two-lane highway that would take them back to town.

He hid a wince as she looked around the interior of his truck. She didn't wrinkle her nose or make any outward sign that riding in the older vehicle bothered her, but he figured she was good at hiding her emotions.

Once again, he reminded himself there wasn't any use in pretending to be something he wasn't.

But it didn't stop him from wishing, just a little, that he could've been someone different. Someone who deserved to be on a date with a princess.

~ * ~

Mia walked next to Ethan, trying not to feel out of place. Trying not to be conspicuous with the two hulking bodyguards following a pace behind them. She hadn't realized her designer jeans and jacket would be so out of place. Everyone else wore what looked like faded work jeans and sweatshirts, though Ethan had texted her that a team sweatshirt wasn't necessary.

She'd meant to talk to Gideon and Alessandra about the level of security. Most days she vacillated between feeling the goon guards were overkill and feeling edgy, like someone could be watching her. But she certainly hadn't meant to lose her temper in front of Ethan.

Something was going on with Gideon and Alessandra. She didn't know what, whether it was something in their relationship or something else, but there had been more than one time that they'd broken off their conversation when she'd entered the room.

She hated feeling like they were keeping secrets from her. But maybe she was being overly sensitive. Maybe it wasn't about her at all.

The crowd entering the outdoor football stadium was a mix of families with moms and dads with kids and teenagers in pairs and threesomes. It was noisy and chaotic, and she loved the energy.

It was also completely different from the last date she'd been on. She and Richard had been at a quiet, private table in an expensive restaurant back home. And look how that had turned out.

She slipped her hand into Ethan's for the second time, partly to keep from getting separated from him in the crowd, but partly to see the slow blush that climbed into his cheeks. He carried a folded fleece blanket in his other arm.

He paid the admission charge, and they continued, swept along with the crowd toward a set of metal bleachers. Her detail followed right behind.

Several people greeted Ethan, one the veterinarian Mia recognized, who was walking beside a teenage girl. Mia noticed the woman's eyebrows go up toward her hairline.

They found a space on the bleachers, and Goon One and Goon Two settled in two rows behind them. She looked around eagerly, taking in the players on the field—lots of them— the bright lights, and the crowd.

"You'll have to explain what's going on to me," she said. "I don't know the rules."

They let go of each other's hands to get settled, and he stuck the blanket between his feet.

"Right now they're just warming up."

Her eyes caught on the cheerleading squad, already pumping up the crowd from below. Several rows of bleachers near the front were filled with uniformed band members, each holding different instruments.

"This is so fun. Thank you for bringing me."

He looked at her askance. "You're serious?"

"Why wouldn't I be?"

He rubbed both hands over his thighs. "This is a high school football game," he said as if she'd somehow missed that fact. "You probably attend events like Wimbledon and the Olympics and—"

"Water polo?" She leaned one elbow on her knee and rested her cheek on her fist. She raised her brows at him. "So I can't be interested in a high school sport?"

He had the good grace to look embarrassed. But then seemed to recover. "What was your last date?"

She wrinkled her nose. "It was a dinner date. And it wasn't a particularly good one."

He didn't ask for more details.

So she went back to the original topic. "Or maybe you think I was looking for any reason to get out from under my sister and Gideon's noses for a few hours?"

He slanted a glance at her, his mouth tight, though not quite a frown. "Were you?"

"Only a little." She nudged his boot with the toe of her shoe. "Is it really so farfetched that I might want to spend time with you?"

He murmured something under his breath and rubbed the back of his neck, expression chagrined.

"What?" she pressed.

He shook his head.

"What was your last date?"

"I haven't dated much. At all." That color was rising in his face again, and she tried not to let it distract her.

"Which is it?" she asked. "Much? Or at all?"

He kept his gaze on the field. A whistle blew, and he let out a small exhale. "That's the referee's whistle. They're starting."

She turned to face the field, aware of the man at her elbow. How could someone like Ethan not have dated? He was handsome, young. She didn't know anything about dairy farming, but it seemed as if he had a strong work ethic.

On the field, players from each team lined up, bent low and forward. One player jogged back and forth behind the line.

The crowd didn't go completely silent, but it seemed to hold its breath. She could hear one of the players, standing behind the line, shouting. She couldn't make out the words.

And then both lines seemed to break at the same moment and rush toward each other. The guy from behind the line somehow had a brown ball in hand and, before she could even register everything that was happening on the field, he threw it to the ground in an empty spot.

The crowd groaned.

"Was that bad?" She glanced at Ethan. His blush had tamed somewhat, but he still kept his eyes on the field, not on her.

"Incomplete pass," Ethan said. "They'll have four downs—it's like four attempts—to get the ball ten or more yards down the field. If they don't make the yards they need, the other team gets the ball."

"Hmm." She watched as the teams lined up again.

The sequence started out the same, with both teams rushing at each other, but this time when she expected the guy behind the line to have the ball, it had disappeared.

The crowd cheered, and Ethan pointed to a young man sprinting down the field just before he was smashed by another, larger player.

She leaned close, her shoulder bumping Ethan's. "Much?" she whispered. "Or at all?"

He shot her a resigned look, one that read, *are you happy now?* "At all."

"Why not?"

~ * ~

Mia's frank question had Ethan stumped. He was getting a little more used to her directness and had—thankfully—stopped blushing so much.

Had he given up on dating too easily? He'd always believed he was too busy, that any girl he was attracted to would reject him because of his financial and family situation.

"I've had custody of my brothers since I was nineteen," he said. "Since my stepmother died."

"Oh. I didn't realize." She bumped his shoulder again, this time a gesture of solidarity. Not that he'd minded the flirtatious way she'd done it before. "That must've been hard for you, taking on all that responsibility at such a young age."

He looked back to the field, where the home team had fumbled the ball and the visitors were setting up offense. Carol had pushed him to run the dairy, to take care of the family like Dad would've wanted, often manipulating him with guilt and tears.

"It wasn't that bad," he said. There had been moments—sometimes very few and far between—where he'd felt close to his stepbrothers. Like the time when the boys had been twelve and thirteen, and the three of them had snuck away for a morning of fishing in the creek.

Those moments had grown much more rare in the last few years. Now...this might be the last time he watched them play, if they couldn't get their grades up. It was a sobering thought.

When he looked back to Mia, she was considering him with what almost looked like admiration.

He averted his eyes. Surely he was imagining that. Seeing what he wanted to see.

"They're going to try a big pass," he said, nodding to the field, hoping to divert her attention.

"How can you tell?"

Okay, he wasn't imagining that she'd edged slightly closer. Where there'd been a couple of inches between their legs, now her jean-clad thigh rested next to his.

"Uhh... See the formation? The way the players are lined up?" He glanced at her, but she just looked more confused. "When they're lined up like that, it usually means they're going to try a long pass."

Maybe she'd moved closer because she was cold. With the sun going down, the breeze was starting to get chilly. That's why he'd brought the blanket.

"Do you come to all your stepbrothers' games?"

He shook his head, trying to clear the fuzz that came from being so close to her. "Just the home games. And I don't always stay until the end. The ladies—the cows—have to be milked twice a day. The first time early in the morning, so it makes for a short night."

"How early?"

"I'm usually in the barn by four."

Her mouth fell open. "But that's still the middle of the night."

"It's technically morning."

She shook her head emphatically. "That's...torture!"

He couldn't help smiling at her emphatic words. "It isn't so bad. You get used to it, after a while." He'd been doing it for so long he couldn't remember anything else.

"Well, I hope your brothers appreciate what you're sacrificing for them."

She'd meant it as a joke, meant the lost sleep he'd never get back. He knew she did, and yet, the words penetrated the careful wall he'd built. He always tried not to think about his brothers and the many ways they'd taken advantage.

What about living your life? The principal's words from earlier in the week echoed in his subconscious and reared their heads at inopportune times. Like now. Did he even have a right to think like that?

"Wow, look at that frown. I'm sorry I brought it up." Mia leaned into him again, her concerned expression drawing him from his funk.

"It's okay." He shrugged, tried to shrug it away, like he usually did. Lately, it was harder to lock those thoughts away where they belonged.

"I guess everybody has difficult family."

He grabbed on to the subject change with both hands. "You too?"

The easy smile faded, and he instantly missed it. She glanced around them, as if just registering the crowd on all sides.

And he realized she was probably worried that what she told him could be overheard and might be spilled to social media or tabloid magazines.

He might tire of the small town grapevine, but he couldn't imagine feeling under a microscope all the time.

"It's okay," he said quickly. "You can tell me later." Or not at all. He'd already experienced so much on this date, he couldn't expect a second one.

She looked slightly relieved. "I'll owe you a favor."

"Do you speak French?" he joked.

"*Mais oui.*"

CHAPTER FOUR

Gideon ran through the Excel spreadsheet once more. He'd been scrolling up and down the screen, staring at columns of numbers for hours, and his head was pounding.

He was trained for combat, could speak six languages, and could build a bomb. But he was no accountant.

Leaning back from where he'd been hunched over the laptop keyboard at the dining room table, he realized evening was falling. He'd been so focused on the computer that he'd missed the entire afternoon.

But after two days of meticulously combing through bank statements and the monthly accounting ledgers, he'd finally found the discrepancy.

Three months ago, while he and Alessandra had been in Glorvaird, there'd been a ten-thousand-dollar withdrawal from the bank. Since then, multiple transactions for expenses had been adjusted, increasing the expense amounts by different amounts, from a hundred dollars to several hundred at a time.

If the adjustments had been a one-time error, or

maybe had occurred twice, he could've chalked it up to a mistake. But the mysterious bank withdrawal and the adjustments to numerous expenditures meant someone was trying to cover their tracks. Someone had stolen from the Triple H.

They'd almost gotten away with it too, since the difference between the bank balance and the transaction register was almost non-existent now. If he hadn't noticed it last week, he could've missed it entirely. That might've opened the door for the thief to steal *more* from his family.

Had the person done it simply because Gideon had been distracted by his new relationship with Alessandra? Because he was traveling part-time with his fiancée?

He didn't want to consider it, but other than his brother and sister, Nate was the only person on the ranch who had access to the bank account. As the foreman, he had to be able to make purchases to run the Triple H. Gideon hated to think that a man he trusted so deeply would do something like this.

But there was also the fact that something had happened between his sister and a hand named Trey. When Gideon and Alessandra had declared their love for each other and decided to make a go of things, it had seemed as if Trey and Carrie had been beginning a relationship. Sometime while Gideon and Alessandra had been in Glorvaird, Trey and Carrie had cooled things off. Gideon didn't know why, and neither the ranch hand nor Carrie was talking. Was there any chance Trey had either conned his sister out of the money or had somehow used her to facilitate the transaction?

With Gideon's brother Matt overseas, that left hands Dan, Brian and Chase as the other suspects. Could any of them have pulled this off?

Until this point, everyone on the Triple H had felt like family. Been trusted as such.

Gideon rubbed his forehead, but it didn't ease the pounding behind his eyes.

"Gideon?" Alessandra said his name, and he looked up, blinking.

She came up behind him, and he blanked the screen, more out of habit than wanting to keep it from her. Her arms came around his shoulders, her cheek pressed into his. "Isn't it about time for a break?"

He nodded, enjoying the rasp of his beard against her cheek, but he couldn't shake the disappointment and anger that weighted him down.

She bussed his cheek with a kiss. "Find something?"

She must've felt him tense up, because she put a few inches between them, no longer teasing and flirty, though she still held on to his shoulders. "You did," she whispered.

"Part of it. I'm waiting on the bank to provide photocopies of the transaction. The manager thought he could pull digital copies of the surveillance cameras, too. I won't know for sure which one of the guys it was until then."

She fell silent. Emotion radiated off of her, and

when she spoke, her voice was quiet but brimming with hurt. "One of the guys? I can't believe any of the cowboys would do that to you."

He was almost one hundred percent sure it was Nate. Nate was the only one with bank access, though the other hands could access the ranch's computer at any time.

He knew Alessandra had found peace and solace here when she'd been on the run from the assassins who'd tried to kill her. The cowboys had been a big part of that. And he felt just the same about the guys. They'd been together a long time. Dan had come to them most recently, and he'd been on the payroll for five years. It wasn't a pleasant feeling to think that someone you counted as family had stabbed you in the back.

He rubbed his fists into his eye sockets but didn't quite dislodge her hands from his shoulders. "Are we making a mistake here?"

She went perfectly still, and he regretted the words as soon as he'd said them. But just because he regretted them didn't mean the thought hadn't been rolling around his head since he'd first discovered there might be a theft.

She let go of him and took several steps away from his chair. She wrapped her arms around her middle in a pose that reminded him of when he'd rejected their relationship—when he'd thought they'd be better off going their separate ways.

This time, the diamond engagement ring sparkled from her left hand.

"What, exactly, do you mean by that?" Her voice was low and even, but he could hear the undertone of hurt.

He stood up, bad knee cracking as he straightened to his full height.

How could he explain this in a way that wouldn't hurt her more? "When someone commits a crime, there's usually this conflagration of three things." He used his index finger to draw a triangle in the air in front of himself. "Need," he ticked off the first side of the triangle. "Rationalization." Ticked the second. "And opportunity." He glanced at her, but it was clear from her puzzled expression that she didn't see where he was going with this. "Me being gone for months at a time opened a door. Whoever did this took advantage."

She nodded slowly, her mouth a flat line that he hated. "Opportunity. I get it. So you think if you'd been here, this wouldn't have happened?"

He shrugged, looked away.

They'd talked before, at length, about his protective tendencies, especially where his sister was concerned. His fears that Carrie and her daughter Scarlett could be hurt or in danger while he was gone overseas were part of the struggle he'd had when he'd wrestled with being with Alessandra in the first place.

He thought he'd overcome the need to be here, on the Triple H. But this situation had brought those fears right back. He couldn't help feeling that if he'd been on the premises, this wouldn't have happened.

Alessandra uncrossed her arms, paced several

steps toward him with arms akimbo. "You weren't on a top secret mission, Gideon. Whoever did this could have picked up the phone and gotten you on your cell at any time. If they were in trouble, they should've asked you for help. Not taken the cash and tried to cover it up. This is *not your fault.*"

He looked at her, forced himself to let go of the stress and guilt and betrayal he'd felt all afternoon, and really looked at the fiery princess, riled up on his behalf. He reached for her, and she came into his arms easily.

He could let go of his tension—some of it at least—but he still couldn't help feeling that this was at least partly his fault. His responsibility. And he'd been gone.

But holding Alessandra close, burying his face in her hair... He couldn't imagine pushing her away a second time, especially not when they were supposed to be celebrating their engagement. She was *his.* She'd agreed to be his wife.

He couldn't let her go, but he also had a responsibility to his family and to the Triple H.

What was he supposed to do now?

~ * ~

"What is that smell?" Robbie asked from his slouched seat at the small kitchen table.

Ethan knew what the smell was. Skunk.

He moved past the boys at the cramped kitchen table in their single-wide and headed for the back door. He only had to crack it to see their golden Labrador, Peanut, sitting at attention just outside, wanting to come in.

And just cracking the door let in more of the awful stink.

He shut the door quickly.

"Did you let Peanut out?" he asked the boy, turning back to the table.

Sam didn't look up from the comic book he had spread across the other end of the table. "I did a while ago."

The boys had an open bag of potato chips and Oreos between them on the tabletop. With both of them and their football bulk slouched there, there was only room left at the very corner.

Ethan was having a hard time picturing Princess Mia seated there.

And an even harder time imagining his brothers behaving politely while she tutored them.

Was this tutoring session just asking for trouble?

When he'd made the teasing comment at the football game last weekend, he'd never expected her to agree to help. He'd even tried to dissuade her, but it seemed once she'd set her mind on it, he wouldn't be able to talk her out of it.

He'd planned to stick close and make sure his brothers showed the proper respect, but with their golden lab smelling up the entire trailer just by sitting on the back porch, he didn't see how he could do that. He could lock Peanut in the dairy barn, but that'd cause him no end of trouble in the morning when the cows revolted against the smell.

"Did you check the back gate?" Ethan pressed Sam. The gate had a faulty latch, and if it didn't get closed tightly, it came open. Now it appeared the dog had gotten out and found a disaster. His brothers' irresponsibility was nothing new, but this timing was the worst.

He could just picture the princess holding a handkerchief over her nose and mouth and trying not to gag as she helped his brothers.

This was a disaster.

A knock sounded at the front door. Crap.

He threw an encompassing glance at them. "Behave. I mean it. Remember, you playing football depends on your grades."

They'd been argumentative and defensive about the incident with their teacher and the subsequent detention. And he'd spoken to them at-length over the past days about what it would mean for their college careers if they didn't get football scholarships, and if they didn't get these grades up.

But now Robbie made a face, as if mimicking Ethan. Sam snorted softly.

Ethan suppressed a sigh. What could he do but open the front door?

It was only a matter of steps in their fifteen-by-seventy-two foot trailer. He'd tried not to think about the disparity between what Mia was used to and what she'd find here. He didn't want to be ashamed of his circumstances, not when he'd fought tooth and nail to provide for his family.

But that didn't stop heat from burning his face as he pulled open the door.

"Hey," he greeted her. One of her security goons was on the step just behind her. At least with someone burly like that on the premises, his stepbrothers weren't likely to get in real trouble.

"I've got a small problem. You can probably smell it."

Her nose scrunched, obscuring her freckles and creating an adorable crinkle between her eyes. "What is it?"

"Skunk. My stepbrothers... My dog got out of the yard and apparently met up with one. Let me introduce you to the boys, then I'll disappear out back to give her a bath. I didn't mean to leave you on your own."

She reached out and touched his forearm, stopping his rushed words. "No worries. Can I come in?"

His face went even hotter as he moved to let her pass. He made quick work of the introductions in the kitchen and then left Mia and her bodyguard inside with his stepbrothers and walked out the back door. He was a little afraid to read in her expression what she really thought of the tiny trailer.

Peanut lay on the edge of the small back deck, her chin on her front paws. When he walked over to her, she looked up at him with morose eyes.

"You're a mess, girl," he said with a sigh.

And then he left the porch behind, casting one last look at the trailer. "And so am I. C'mon."

A half hour later, he wasn't sure who'd gotten the bigger bath, him or Peanut. After a tomato juice rinse and two shampoos, she smelled moderately better. Of course, she'd shaken excess shampoo and water all over him numerous times, when his reflexes hadn't been fast enough to stop her.

Now *he* smelled like wet dog.

He'd taken off the worn chambray over-shirt that had borne the brunt of most of the soaking and now wore a T-shirt and jeans that were only *mostly damp*.

Half of the deck was bathed in late afternoon sunlight, and Peanut lay stretched out on her side, soaking up its warmth. He stood nearby, leaning against the railing with his arms crossed.

Should he go inside? There would be no sneaking past his stepbrothers or the princess. The place was too small for them not to notice when he opened the back door. But at least he could clean up a little in his bedroom, get a clean, dry shirt.

Before he'd had time to think a decision all the way through, the back door opened and Robbie's head poked out. "Hank's here. Sam and me're going to hang with the guys for a while."

"Wait!" Their friends were here? This tutoring session had been planned for three days! Ethan squared off toward the door. "What about your tutoring? Mia came out here to help you two. You can't just run off."

"It's been like a half hour, Ethan. We're bored, and we're going."

Before Ethan could take more than a half-step

toward the house, Robbie had slammed the door closed, leaving Ethan outside, alone.

Frustrated. And embarrassed by his stepbrothers' actions.

He ran one hand through his hair, bracing himself to go inside and apologize.

He was reaching out for the door when it opened again, this time Mia danced outside and almost right into his arms.

He jerked back up a step. Didn't know if she saw his fumble as she turned to make sure the door latched.

"I guess they're already gone?" He didn't really have much hope that they'd stayed, not since she'd come outside.

"Yes."

He rubbed the back of his neck with one hand. "I'm sorry if they were rude to you."

"They weren't really," she said, and he narrowed his eyes, trying to gauge whether she was stretching the truth. "They weren't all that attentive."

He exhaled, frustration with his brothers and embarrassment warring in him. "I'm sorry," he said again.

She shrugged, and smiled. "It's all right. I really came to see you, anyway." She rendered him speechless and open-mouthed as she turned to look at Peanut. With her back turned, he could admire her knee-length skirt, the tights, and the slate-colored sweater that hugged her curves.

"Is this the guy—"

"Gal," he managed in a strangled voice.

She gave him a sassy *look* over her shoulder. "The *lady* that got attacked by a mean old skunk?"

Peanut raised her head, tail thumping the wood deck beneath her. When she realized Mia was approaching, the dog got to her feet.

He cleared his throat, tried to find some shred of dignity. "She probably hunted it down. That one has a nose for getting into trouble."

"Aw, she seems sweet."

Peanut sat obligingly to be petted, almost as regal as Mia was as the princess scratched behind her ears and beneath her chin.

"She is," he agreed. "Mostly."

"Hmm." This time when she glanced over her shoulder, an ornery smile lit her eyes. "Like her owner."

~ * ~

Mia knew she shouldn't take such pleasure in seeing that blush climb in Ethan's cheeks, but she couldn't help herself.

The dog's fur was soft and damp beneath her hands, and she gave the animal one last pat before she turned to Ethan. She'd already asked her security detail to wait in the car.

"I believe I promised you some of my secrets," she said.

She didn't really want to divulge her family's drama to Ethan, but fair was fair, and she wasn't ready to head back to the Triple H yet. Something had happened between Gideon and Alessandra two days ago. They were still engaged, still apparently happy, but there was some tension between them, and Alessandra wasn't talking.

It made for long, quiet evenings on her own.

"You don't owe me anything," Ethan said. He settled against the railing in a loose-limbed, relaxed pose.

And that was just another thing to like about the dairy farmer. He didn't keep count of favors owed. There was no scale to balance, like her former boyfriend, the duke of Regis, who'd always expected something from her.

Ethan was like no one she'd ever met before. Last Friday night, when the wind had turned cold, he'd tucked her into the fleece blanket he'd brought along.

It had taken her ten minutes to talk him into sharing the blanket, when his hands had been white with cold as he'd tried to tuck them into his jacket pockets. And when the blanket had been wrapped around both of their shoulders, enclosing them in warmth, she'd waited.

He hadn't tried anything. Hadn't put his arm around her. Hadn't held her hand. Hadn't tried to sneak a kiss.

None of the men she knew would've missed a chance like that.

His hesitation had made her lean into him on Friday, blaming the blanket for the need to be close, when really, it had been all her.

She knew he was attracted to her. At least, she thought so. Even if she discounted the blushes as something else—embarrassment or humility—every once in a while, she caught him looking at her with an intensity that could only be attraction.

Was he really that honorable? Or did something else hold him back?

She settled next to him at the railing, close enough that their shoulders brushed, but she faced outward.

"This is really pretty," she said, getting her first long look at his property. A long, low white barn was nestled into the landscape across the way. A white rail fence spread back onto the property, and black and white cows dotted green fields beyond.

"Thank you." He turned to match her stance, though he stood straight while she leaned against the railing. "But it's nothing like it used to be when my dad was alive."

His words were even, but she heard the underlying emotion.

"My stepmother was forced to sell off quite a bit of our land. Which means we don't have enough grazing pasture for full capacity. Which means it's hard to make a profit. You can see there are repairs that need to be made but..." *We can't afford it.* She heard the words he didn't say.

She saw that the barn needed to be painted. And some of the fence drooped, as if it needed to be replaced.

Ethan sounded defeated. It was slight, but there. The inside of his family's trailer was older, out of date. Tiny. The entire thing was smaller than many hotel rooms she'd stayed in before.

But everything was neat and tidy. She remembered herself as a teen—all right, and sometimes now—how her clothes ended up all over the place. Of course the palace had staff that cooked and cleaned up after the royal family. Ethan managed it all himself. Without, it seemed, much help from his stepbrothers.

"I think it's amazing what you've done for your family, all on your own."

He shook his head slightly, but she persisted. "It *is*."

He didn't make another denial, but she saw the twist of his lips that said he didn't think he was amazing at all.

They stood in comfortable silence for a few moments. She sighed. "My family can also be...difficult."

She didn't like to talk about it. Had barely broached the subject with the men she'd dated before. But somehow, Ethan's patience as he waited for her to elaborate made it easier to keep going.

She told him all of it. Father's MS diagnosis when she'd been ten and feeling that she didn't really know the man, only the crown. Eloise's near-fatal car accident years ago and how it had turned her sister into a beastly person. That she and Alessandra didn't have the close relationship that she wanted.

The only thing she didn't tell him was her dating past. She was a little ashamed of how easily she'd let herself fall in love with those other men.

Though in the face of her deepening feelings for Ethan, she wasn't sure she could call those old flings love. Not really. Now, her previous feelings seemed more like infatuation.

Somehow, while she'd been talking, Ethan's hand had closed over hers on the railing. She'd been the one to link their fingers together, wanting the closeness of that more intimate clasp.

He didn't offer her platitudes, just held on.

Alessandra's engagement ball was ten days away. At Eloise's prodding, Mia had promised she would come home soon after.

But how could she just walk away from someone as special as Ethan? She wanted to see him again.

Now she leaned toward him, pressing into his shoulder and looking up at him. Their hands remained linked.

"Are you planning to come to the engagement ball?" she asked softly.

He exhaled what might've been a bit of a laugh, his lips twisting until he looked down on her and must've realized she was serious.

"Me?" He seemed incredulous.

"Yes, you." She bumped him with her hip. "Everyone's invited."

"Everyone like the *governor* of Texas and *Brad Pitt* and..." He raised his eyebrows as if daring her to contradict him. Or to go on with the list, she wasn't sure.

And she realized she desperately wanted him

there. He would be the only real friend in a sea of people who wanted things from her. There'd be press, who'd already started sniffing around town, looking for more news about *the kissing princess.*

"I think Brad declined the invitation. Which is really too bad." Her lips quirked. She turned toward him, still clinging to his hand, which forced him to face her as well.

"Please, will you come? For me?"

He stared down at her, and she couldn't decipher his expression. Uncertainty? Confusion?

"There'll be dancing, right? The fancy kind, like...waltzing?" He asked it as if he didn't even know if waltz was the right term. He shrugged slightly, almost helplessly. "I don't know how to dance like that."

"Well, then. I'll show you."

~ * ~

Ethan had only meant to find an excuse—any excuse—for Mia to rescind her invitation to her sister's engagement ball, but instead he found himself with his arms full of slender woman.

This was...uncomfortable. She was too close, and he was afraid he still smelled like wet dog.

It was also heaven.

The sun had set while she'd talked about her family, sharing with him in a way that no one had since his dad had died. Now only a sliver of light showed on the western horizon, and the flood light halfway between the barn and house was the only other illumination. Every once in a while a car passed on the two-lane road out front.

It made things feel more intimate than they probably should have. He breathed shallowly, wondering if he should call this off completely.

She stepped back slightly and touched his shoulders, then ran her small hands along his upper arms, positioning them the way she wanted. Then she pushed down.

He lowered his arms, thinking that's what she wanted, but she *tsked* at him. "No, no. You've got to have strong arms to lead your partner. Not noodle arms. Try again."

He raised his arms back to where she'd had them, and this time when she pushed down against him, he resisted her and kept his arms in place.

"Good." When she smiled up at him like that, he felt about ten feet tall.

And then she stepped forward, into the circle of his arms, and his brain and ability to speak floated right out of the top of his head.

She tucked his right hand around the curve of her waist before resting her left hand on his shoulder. Her other hand came up to clasp his.

His mouth was so dry he couldn't tell her that this was a recipe for disaster and that they'd better stop now.

They were so close that her temple brushed his chin as she settled fully into his arms. He swallowed hard.

"The waltz is a simple pattern," she said softly, as if she sensed the intimacy of the moment as well. "One, two, three. One, two, three. Pretend we're standing in a box. You're the man, you'll lead. That means you'll move forward, and I'll follow you."

"And you're just going to trust me not to let you run into anything?" It seemed dangerous to let a man guide her backwards.

"I said 'pretend we're in a box.' We won't be moving that much. Let's try it. Your left foot first. One, two, three. One, two—" *Oof.* She stifled the sound.

He froze.

He'd stepped on her foot.

He winced. "Sorry." He glanced down to see what kind of shoes she was wearing, what kind of damage he might've done to her toes.

"I'm fine." Her hand came off his shoulder, and he thought she might step away, but she chucked him beneath his jaw. "Chin up. Eyes up. Again. One, two, three."

He didn't step on her foot this time, moving slowly to prevent it from happening.

She stopped him with a hand to his chest. "You're a half step behind the count, now. You have to follow the music—"

"What music?"

She thumped him on the chest, a silent reprimand. "Don't worry that you're going to step on me. Trust that I'll follow your lead."

She looked up at him fiercely, and the stubborn

tilt of her chin made his stomach flip and his heart pound. *I'll follow your lead.* Surely, she'd meant the words literally. He was the only one reading into this. He had to be.

This time when she counted the beats off, he squinted his eyes almost closed, not wanting to see her face if he did step on her again. He did as she asked, trusted her count, and this time, they completed the square with no mishaps.

She made him do it again, smiling up at him like he'd accomplished something fantastic, instead of a simple dance step. He'd started to relax infinitesimally when she said, "Good. Now let's add a turn."

He didn't fumble it too badly. She made him do it again.

The moon started to come up, lending a silver glimmer to her skin and a luminescence to her eyes as she gazed up at him.

"At the ball I'll be wearing a gown with a huge skirt," she said. "So it will make it slightly more difficult to maneuver. But you'll also have less chance of stepping on my feet."

She spoke as if he'd already agreed to go. As if she'd actually want to dance with him if he did go. He hadn't been joking about the caliber of the other guests. No way would he fit in there. But if she wanted him there...

She let go of his shoulder and spun out in a turn beneath his upraised arm, laughing. The spirited, free sound went straight to his heart. When she twirled back to him, he went still.

She met him there, resting her free hand on his chest. He still had her other hand clasped in his. He drew it to his chest, just above his heart.

She was bright, like a diamond shining up at him from his arms.

He couldn't breathe.

Her eyes were large, and he thought maybe he should let her go, except then her gaze flicked down to his mouth and held there for a protracted moment.

Did she want him to kiss her?

The outrageous thought twirled through his mind in the same way she'd spun in his arms. It made him just as wobbly.

Then she leaned toward him slightly. Maybe raised up on her tiptoes.

He only had instinct to go on and lowered his head. His pulse pounded in his temples and he was really going to kiss—

Suddenly, she pushed away from his embrace, and he released her instantly.

Cool autumn air rushed into the space between their bodies, and as she turned from him, the flood light illuminated the stricken expression on her face.

Heat and humiliation pounded through him with every beat of his heart. "I'm sorry," he said.

"No, it wasn't—" *You.*

Wasn't that something people said when it *was* you? His inexperience hampered him, but it stood to reason he'd misread all of her cues. He'd only imagined her leaning toward him, imagined her glance at his lips.

She tucked a lock of hair behind her ear. "I need to go."

He cleared his throat. "Yes, all right."

He trailed her around the trailer and through the chain-link gate, mind grasping for what to say. Should he apologize again?

Then she got in the car with her security goon, offering only a subdued goodbye before the door clunked closed.

He was afraid of what she'd think if he stood there watching her drive away, so he gave a lame wave and turned to climb the trailer steps.

Inside, he leaned his shoulder against the closed door, breaths harsh and loud in the stillness.

Had he just ruined the first real friendship he'd had since his dad?

CHAPTER FIVE

"Do you like how this looks?"

Alessandra's question drew Mia's head up from her phone. She'd been trying to decide whether she should text Ethan or not.

She gazed at her sister in the triplicate mirrors of the trendy, upscale Dallas boutique. Alessandra wore a floor-length, pale pink gown with a ruched skirt and an off-the-shoulders design.

They were the only ones in the dressing room this afternoon. At Gideon's insistence, they'd paid well for privacy, and the shop had closed to other customers for a few hours. Several smaller doors led off the mirrored main area, where multiple women could dress at the same time and then come out to admire themselves. Mia sat on one of the two small sofas that bracketed the wood floor and made it more welcoming.

"It's beautiful," Mia told her sister.

"That's a cop-out answer." Alessandra twirled to stare at her hips in the mirror. "It makes me look huge here." She motioned with both hands to her *derrière*.

"It's the way the skirt fits, it's not you. Anyone can see that." This was the sixth gown Alessandra had rejected.

And maybe Mia was a little distracted. It had been two days since she'd practically run out of Ethan's arms, and she was still spooked.

She'd almost kissed the man. Completely forgotten about her promise until the very last second.

She'd *wanted* his kiss. Desperately. Ardently.

"What is with you?" Alessandra complained as she slipped out of the dress. The stylist quickly and quietly took it from her, leaving Mia's sister in her slip and underwear as she waited for the next in line.

Mia blinked back the hot feeling in her eyes. "Nothing."

Alessandra crossed her arms. "Now you're lying to me. If you don't want to talk about your farmer-boy, fine, but you don't have to lie."

Mia's chin went up. "I don't want to talk about Ethan."

She didn't want to keep remembering the hurt that had pierced his eyes just before he'd shuttered his entire expression. Or how quick he'd been to say, *I'm sorry*.

The whole thing had been her fault.

She couldn't face the swirling thoughts. She stood up abruptly. "And if you want to talk about lying, why don't you let me in on the big secret that you've been holding onto since Glorvaird?"

Color leached out of Alessandra's face. "What?"

Mia was shaking now, but she couldn't stop the words from spewing forth. "You and Gideon keep having conversations that stop when I walk in the room. You haven't looked me in the eye since we left the palace."

Alessandra's gaze skittered away. The stylist started to come back into the room, her arms full of tulle, but Alessandra waved her off. She ducked away.

Alessandra pressed her hands together in front of her waist, a sign of tension that Mia knew and recognized. She waited her sister out.

After a long exhale, Alessandra looked her in the eye. "Father told Eloise about an—an affair. From when we were small. We have a half-sister somewhere in the states. Eloise asked me to find her. She dropped off the grid years ago."

Mia sat back down, stunned. That was the last thing she'd expected. She'd known there was a secret, but she hadn't given real thought to what it was.

An affair? A missing half-sister?

"When were you going to tell me?" She forced the words out past lips that felt numb.

Alessandra shrugged, her hands pressing together so hard her knuckles were white. "I was trying to figure out the best time."

Mia stood up, unable to keep looking at her sister. Betrayal fired through her veins and tears threatened. "I'll wait in the car."

"Mia—"

But she didn't wait to hear whatever else

Alessandra was going to say.

~ * ~

Two days after the kiss that wasn't, Ethan was worn slick. The one thing he wanted most was to fall into bed and forget the last three days had happened.

He still couldn't reconcile what had happened those last few minutes he and Mia had been together.

But he also couldn't forget the look on her face when she'd asked him to go to the ball.

Was he crazy to even consider going? He knew he'd stick out like a mutt in a room full of Persian cats, but even so, he'd dug to the very back of his closet, to the box of his dad's things that Carol hadn't thrown away or sold. There wasn't much. A ball glove. A handful of baseball cards that had sentimental value.

And his dad's suit.

Ethan had shrugged into the charcoal-gray suit coat to test the fit and found that he must have the same body shape as Dad, because it fit perfectly.

Now he sat on the end of his bed and looked at the suit that he'd hung up in the doorway to his closet.

It was a timeless style, a simple cut, but even so, it looked dated. But Ethan had paid the electric bill and water bill earlier today and knew there was no money for a frivolous expense like a tuxedo rental, not if he and the boys wanted to eat.

It would do, and hopefully it wouldn't shame Mia

too much if he wore it.

It wasn't as if he expected her to stay by his side during the fancy event. No doubt there would be expectations of her, since her sister was the guest of honor, and he knew she was helping manage the event.

Besides, she'd been completely silent on text messages since she'd run off the property Tuesday night. He'd gotten used to receiving one or two texts from her a day, little messages that were more friendly than anything.

That she hadn't texted him in two days was telling.

Maybe she regretted inviting him. Maybe she didn't want him to attend at all.

"Ethan!" Sam's voice rang out from the hallway.

Ethan wanted to ignore him, wanted to throw his arm over his eyes and lie down on the bed, but Sam burst in the door without waiting for an invitation to come in.

"There's nothing to eat."

He took a breath before answering. "Where's Robbie? You guys can borrow the truck and head to the store."

Sam shrugged. "Somewhere off with Hank and his buddies. I'm dying here."

Ethan knew that his brother would keep whining if he didn't get what he wanted. Maybe it was taking the easy way out, but he got in his truck and headed to the grocery store.

An hour later, he'd worked his way through the shopping and was finally on the home stretch. The checkout stand.

Of course, there were only two checkers and three people in both lines, and so he was barely holding on to his patience as he inched up to the conveyor belt.

And his eyes caught on a familiar face on the cover of one of the tabloids in the checkout stand rack.

Mia.

He looked away immediately, forcing his eyes to the bright afternoon sunlight streaming through the front window panes. Someone had painted an ad on the large glass, but it was faded and chipped off.

He didn't want to know why Mia was featured on a tabloid cover. He didn't.

But he couldn't keep his gaze from drifting back to the magazine.

It was a grainy picture, but he could clearly make out her features as she sat across a small table from a man in a suit and tie. They were holding hands. His eyes went to the caption.

The Kissing Princess.

That was her nickname? He felt as if ice trickled down his spine. *The kissing princess?* Really? When she'd pushed away from him the moment he'd even thought about kissing her?

Heart thumping, he knew he should look away from the magazine, but he couldn't. He edged slightly closer so he could read the print beneath the caption.

Two former beaus fight to win the princess back—who will win her heart at the upcoming engagement ball?

Two who? Men she'd dated? Men she'd been in

love with? The tabloid seemed to indicate these men would be at the big engagement ball. One was a...he squinted at the small print...duke. The other one was a popular international soccer player.

Ethan closed his eyes.

Who was he kidding, thinking she could be attracted to him? These guys were... There was no competition. He wasn't even in the same stadium—the same hemisphere as a duke or a pro soccer player.

"Hon, you ready?" The checker's voice cut through his mental fog, and he started loading his groceries onto the conveyor belt. He moved numbly, kept his eyes downcast on the food, on giving his hands something to do.

He'd tried to stay realistic about being Mia's friend, done his best not to read anything other than friendship into her desire to spend time with him.

Where exactly would things go, even if she were interested in him romantically? She was a *princess*! He was stuck here taking care of his stepbrothers for at least another two years. Even after that, what could he offer her? A piddling living operating a dairy?

What a laugh.

He paid for his groceries and pushed his cart into the parking lot.

And his cell phone dinged the text message chime from his pocket.

Mia: I need to see you.

His hands shook as he stuffed the phone back into his jeans' pocket. He was still raw from the other night, from her withdrawal.

And what he'd read in the tabloid somehow made things worse.

He didn't know whether he could answer her or not. He loaded the groceries in his truck and drove home.

~ * ~

When Ethan pulled into the drive, his headlights swept across the front of the trailer, and he spotted a small figure huddled on the front step.

Mia.

Her arms were wrapped around her knees, and her hair cascaded down her shoulders in a golden stream.

His stomach flipped, and he scrambled to find some sense of equilibrium. He hadn't answered her text, so hadn't expected to see her.

Where was her security escort? He craned his neck to see a headlight and part of the bumper of what looked like a farm truck hidden near the barn, further down his drive. Had she somehow ditched them?

What was going on?

He stepped out of the vehicle and filled his arms with two bags of groceries from the truck bed. Maybe if he kept things short, she'd leave. He was exhausted. Had already dealt with his stepbrothers enough for one day. He didn't know whether he could face more rejection from her.

But when he reached the step and got a good look at her in the twilight, he saw the silver tear tracks down her cheeks.

And the tension he'd been holding slid away in a wave of worry.

He set the grocery bags on the top step and reached for her. "Mia. What's wrong?"

She came off the steps and into his arms. She shook, still crying. Tucked her face into his chest.

Whatever had happened, it had obviously hurt her badly.

And he was man enough to push aside his own hurts.

He held her, letting her get the emotion out.

After a moment, she moved back slightly, using both hands to wipe moisture from her face.

He let her lead. When she sat on the step again, he sat next to her, leaving the groceries on the ground. His frozen foods would last, for now. He didn't hear Sam moving around inside. Maybe his stepbrother was into a video game or something. If he was that hungry, he could come outside and unload the groceries himself.

Mia inhaled, her breath shaky, still unsteady. "Sorry."

His own throat was thick from emotion. "My dad told me it was okay to cry."

She smiled a watery small smile.

Remembering those last days was still painful, though muted now by the years.

"What's going on?" he asked.

And then words burst from her like another flood. A half-sister she'd never known about, her older sisters keeping secrets.

She was hurt. Felt betrayed.

And even if he couldn't identify with her feelings exactly, he could remember the emotions he'd experienced when Dad had died. He put his arm around her shoulders, wanting to comfort.

And that seemed to set her off again. Her sniffle turned into a soft sob. Her face crumpled, and she turned into his shoulder.

"I-I don't even d-deserve for you to be s-so nice to me!" she wailed, her words muffled in his shirt.

This time her sobs abated more quickly, and she sat back again, though still tucked into his arm.

"I'd like to explain," she said after a hiccough.

He shook his head, and his chin brushed her hair. "You don't owe me anything." And he meant it.

"Well, I'm going to anyway." The stubborn tilt of her chin told him she was on her way to recovering from her shock. "You've been a good friend to me. Better than anyone else."

She breathed in deeply, a little steadier now. "About a month ago, I made a promise to myself."

She looked down, her hair falling over her cheek and blocking his view of her eyes.

He waited.

"I promised I wasn't going to kiss anyone again until I was sure it was the man I would marry. You see, I have this habit of falling in love too easily. With the wrong guys."

The bottom dropped out of his stomach. What was she saying? Was she admitting he was a wrong guy?

He forced himself to listen.

"My sisters have always been close to each other. And my father has always been distant. Since I was a teenager and started realizing what love could be, I wanted it. Wanted someone to love me just for me, not for my crown or for what benefits a relationship could bring them. I wanted someone who just wanted me," she finished in a whisper.

The depth of her desire was evident, though she wouldn't look at him, and he couldn't see her eyes.

"And every time I thought I'd fallen for someone who was right, it turned out not to be all wrong. They all just wanted something from me."

What a horrible feeling, to believe the person you loved was using you.

"And every time it happened, I realized I'd given too much of myself to those—to the men I thought I loved. So I promised myself, no more kissing."

Now it made sense why she'd pulled away. She had this vow to uphold.

He swallowed hard. He didn't know if Mia lumped him in the category with those other jerks, but he did know one thing. None of them deserved her. And he would never push for what she wasn't ready to give.

He squeezed her shoulders lightly. She tipped her head and tucked into the space between his neck and shoulder, apparently spent.

He just held her, trying to ignore the pounding of

his heart.

Mia might put off a joyful, vivacious personality, but there were hurts beneath that he'd never expected.

He'd been wrong to want something from her. All she needed was a friend.

I promised I wouldn't kiss anyone... Unless it was the man I planned to marry.

He would never be that man. A princess would never marry someone as dirt poor as he, someone with no prospects.

But he could be the friend she thought he already was.

~ * ~

Alessandra sat in the darkened living room, curled into the couch.

Mia had refused to speak to her on the long ride home from Dallas, ignoring every overture and only looking out the window.

After a few tries, Alessandra had given up.

She'd messed things up with Mia.

The awful thing was, she probably felt a lot of the same things her sister felt. Betrayed by her father. Hurt.

And then there were the questions. Had her mother known, before she'd died? Why hadn't they been enough for Father?

What was their sister like? Did she know about them?

Mostly, Alessandra felt guilty. She blamed herself for not telling Mia sooner. She should've told her sister back in Glorvaird, or even better, forced Eloise to bring her into their chat when Alessandra had found out.

Weren't their relationships fractured enough? She'd known keeping secrets wouldn't be healthy for them, but she'd done it anyway.

She was so stupid.

The light went on in the hall, and she shrank even further into the couch, hoping that whoever it was— one of the cowboys, probably—would pass on by without seeing her.

"Alessandra?"

No luck. Gideon strode into the room, as if he'd sensed her hiding there. Should've gone up to her bedroom while she'd had the chance.

Things had been strained between them since the other night.

Are we making a mistake here? he'd asked.

And it had broken something inside her, hearing those words. She'd been blissfully happy.

Ignorant maybe. Hadn't had an inkling that Gideon continued to struggle with leaving his family behind for months at a time.

Again, she felt stupid. How could she not have realized?

Gideon's protective nature had been one of the things about him she'd first fallen for. He'd made her feel safe, even when she'd been running for her life.

It wasn't realistic to think he'd be able to just turn

it off, even though he'd made a huge sacrifice to be a part of her life.

She didn't think she'd made a noise, but he rounded the couch and came right to her.

He sat next to her, not quite touching.

She stretched the sleeves of her long-sleeved T-shirt to cover her hands and used the material to wipe beneath her eyes.

"Allie-girl," he said roughly, the nickname he rarely used.

"I'm okay." She tried to put on a brave face. She went for a smile, but she felt it wobble a bit.

She knew Gideon had put enormous pressure on himself to find the thief. He was worried about Carrie, too. She didn't want to add to his burden.

But his big, warm palm came to rest at her lower back. He exerted gentle pressure, pulling her to him and, weak as she was, she crawled into his embrace.

"I heard from one of the security detail that you and Mia had a fight," he said into the crown of her head. "She found out about the missing princess?"

She nodded, misery leaching over her anew.

He held her for a long time, not speaking. Then, finally, "I'm sorry for how all this played out."

Her stomach clenched into a tight little ball. Was he going to say that being with her wasn't worth all the trouble? Had be given up on them?

"This theft really hit me hard, and I've handled things all wrong. Especially with you. I'm sorry."

She couldn't help the tears that welled in her eyes, though she wished she could stem them.

She swallowed back a sob. "I'm sorry I didn't realize you were still struggling with the reality of being with me."

"I'm not." He said the words instantly, as if it were his gut reaction. It made her feel marginally better.

He exhaled, his breath ruffling the fine hair at her temple. "If I'd had my head on straight in the beginning... If I hadn't made excuses when you told me you wanted to be together, you wouldn't have a question in your mind right now. I don't regret choosing you, Allie-girl. I love you."

Hearing his words made her tear up again. "I love you too," she said through a tight throat.

"We'll get things figured out here," he said. "Maybe make some changes about how things are run. Everything will settle down."

She should be reassuring him, but he was doing that for her.

"Whatever you need from me," she told him, "I'm here."

He squeezed her lightly. "Mia will come around."

She hoped so. She needed to heal the rift with her sister.

CHAPTER SIX

Late afternoon, the day of the ball, Ethan wrapped up with the dairy cows. He was filthy and in desperate need of a shower.

And there was a small part of him that was excited. Anticipating seeing Mia in her fine ball gown.

Over the past week, the couple of texts they'd shared each day had escalated into phone calls. Sometimes hours-long calls that had him staying up past his usually-early bedtime.

He found he didn't miss the sleep.

After her revelation about the vow she'd made, they'd kept things carefully in the *Friend Zone*. There had been no more practice dances. No more embraces.

She'd told him all about her life in Glorvaird. About her passion for working with battered women. That she couldn't cook a bit. He'd told her everything he remembered about his dad. About how difficult it had been to give up his college dreams. That he'd always wanted to be a veterinarian, but probably never would.

She was the best friend he'd ever had.

And he hadn't been able to keep from falling in love with her. He never planned to tell her. It just was. Part of him, intrinsic to his being.

He loved Princess Mia.

He made his way from the dairy barn to the trailer, pausing to give Peanut a belly rub at the back porch.

He could hear the boys tussling inside before he opened the back door. They'd been edgy and difficult all week. He'd tried talking to them. Tried to bring up the tutoring again with no results.

He sighed, hand on the doorknob. He'd told them he'd be gone for the evening, and they'd had their laugh at his expense. Like everyone else in town, they'd seen the tabloids and knew that Mia had rich, famous suitors at her neck and call. They couldn't understand his friendship with the princess, but that didn't matter to him.

Mia had asked him to go tonight, so he would.

He opened the door to see Robbie take down Sam in a combination football tackle and chokehold—except Sam was wearing a familiar gray suit coat.

Was that—?

"No!" Ethan shouted as he watched in horror. Amidst his brothers wrestling, one sleeve ripped completely off of his father's suit coat.

Robbie and Sam straightened. Neither had the good grace to look abashed. From where he stood, Ethan could see the inside lining of the jacket hanging loose, torn in two places.

The suit pants were crumpled on the floor, a discarded chocolate bar melting atop them, no doubt staining the material irrevocably.

"Are you—? What the—?" He couldn't even get a fell sentence out past the knot of anger lodged in his throat.

"What did you do?" he finally managed.

"Aw, Eeth," Sam said. "We saw this hanging in your closet and thought it would be fun to try it on."

He fisted his hands at his sides, shaking from the rush of adrenaline and anger and despair. "You knew I was planning to go to Mia's ball tonight."

Robbie laughed. Actually laughed. "You were planning to wear that old junk suit?"

"It was my dad's," Ethan said.

"Uh, yeah," Robbie said, "and it's way outta style."

Ethan was unable to find words. No matter if they disagreed with the style or would laugh at him all day long, the suit was *his*. Not theirs. What right did they have to touch it? None.

"After everything I've done for you, everything I've given you—*this* is how you repay me?"

Robbie laughed again, a cruel sound. "Everything you've given us? Like what? This dingy trailer and rice and beans five times a week? Like how you can't even afford to get us a truck of our own? And how you constantly nag us to clean up and do our homework? You call that taking care of us?"

The words hit Ethan like a physical punch. Before he could respond, Robbie said, "C'mon Sam."

He jerked his thumb to the door, and Sam followed him, discarding the ruined suit coat on the floor as he did so.

They left, and the silence that remained seemed deafening.

Ethan moved on numb legs to pick up the pants and suit coat. He knew before looking that there was no way they could be repaired, even if he had more than the two hours before the ball was scheduled to start.

He laid them out on the worn sofa anyway.

And felt like crying. This suit was one of the last things he had of his father, and it was utterly ruined. Completely demolished.

It wasn't just the suit, it was losing his dad. Losing the dream of the life he'd wanted.

Suddenly, the unfairness of it all pressed down on him. No matter Robbie's rude, ungrateful words, Ethan knew he'd done his best by the boys. So what if they ate simple meals? At least they ate. They had a roof over their heads, even if it was a mobile home and not a fancy brick house.

Still shaking with anger and hurt, he made his way out of the front door and sat on the stoop, where he'd sat with Mia a week ago, where he'd promised himself to be her friend and not to expect more.

If he didn't show up at the ball, she was going to be disappointed. Maybe even hate him a little, since he'd promised to be there. He'd be just as bad as the other men who'd let her down.

She was heading back to Glorvaird in a couple of days. Tonight was one of his last chances to see her. Who knew when she'd come back again.

His stepbrothers had ruined everything.

He clutched his head in his hands, pressed his elbows to his knees. Stared at the step between his work boots, trying to figure out some kind of solution.

The sound of tires on gravel drew his gaze up. Whoever it was, he wasn't in the mood for company.

He was shocked to recognize the veterinarian's work truck.

She met him near the steps. "Doesn't look like you're getting all gussied up for that fancy party."

He shrugged helplessly. "You heard about that, huh?"

"You left your phone on the back counter in the office earlier in the week. I might've seen a text from your princess about it. What's keeping you from it?"

His princess. Oh, how he wished.

He went inside and brought the ripped jacket and soiled pants out, held them up for her to see.

"Wow. Your stepbrothers?"

He nodded miserably.

But there was a suspicious twinkle in her eyes as she went back to her truck and ducked inside the driver's side door. "I had my suspicions that those two might try to ruin this for you," she called over her shoulder.

She had? He hadn't seen it coming at all.

And then, "That's why I brought this."

She turned and lifted a garment hanging inside transparent plastic. A tuxedo.

His heart starting beating again. "What's this?"

"James"—her adult son—"bought it for his

wedding and hasn't used it since. I borrowed it. And these." She held up a pair of black dress boots, slicked and shiny in the afternoon light. "Y'all are about the same size."

His throat tightened. "I can't—"

"It's on *loan*." She moved forward and thrust the garment bag into his hands, leaving him no choice but to take it.

"Thank you." She couldn't know how much this meant to him. That someone had noticed. That she'd gone out of her way to make this kind gesture.

She'd saved his day.

Maybe she did know, because her eyes now held a twinkle that looked suspiciously like unshed tears. "And Ethan? Comb your hair."

~ * ~

Gideon waited with Alessandra in a small dressing room upstairs in the McMansion they'd rented out for the ball.

An engagement ball. He'd known better than to argue about it, knew that because of his fiancée's royal blood, there would be expectations.

He'd just as soon have gotten together with their closest friends and had a party over a pile of wings or grilled hamburgers.

"It's packed out there." Alessandra turned from where she'd been peeking through a crack in the outer door, closing it softly behind her. The huge skirt of her royal blue dress swished softly as she moved toward him. She smoothed it nervously, her long white gloves contrasting with the dark fabric.

He'd only seen her in a tiara once before, but she wore one tonight, with her hair swept up in a complicated twist high on her head. Her shoulders were bare and showed off a glittering sapphire necklace that probably cost more than his entire spread.

"That's good, right?" He'd bulked up the event security with a team he'd assembled from local law enforcement and some SEAL friends who were on leave and able to help him out.

He couldn't resist checking his phone. No new messages, which should mean everything was running like it should be. No one had tried to hop the security fence. Nothing suspicious was showing up on the series of security cameras he'd spent the week installing.

He slipped the phone back into the inside breast pocket of his jacket, but not before he caught Alessandra's frown. "Sorry," he said, with an unrepentant grin. Maybe he'd gone overboard, but he refused to take chances, not after what'd happened to Alessandra before.

"Do you remember the steps to our dance?" she pressed.

He moved forward, pant legs brushing against the hem of her dress as he got close enough to take her gloved hand.

"Stop worrying." He gave her hand a squeeze.

They'd had a private instructor visit the Triple H,

and he'd learned a complicated waltz over the past two weeks. Here in a bit, when all the guests had arrived, Mia would announce them as a couple, and they'd make a grand entrance down a wide, curving staircase that led to the ground floor of the mansion. Three large ballrooms emptied into the grand foyer, every surface covered with marble. He and Alessandra would have a special dance together and then, according to his future bride, all he had to do was stand in a receiving line with her and greet their guests. Maybe mingle a bit later. Shake hands and smile.

He wasn't sure he believed it would be that easy, but he'd worked difficult missions and intended to see this one through.

Alessandra smiled tremulously at him. "Are you sure—really sure—you don't want to back out? We haven't been seen together publicly before now, so if there's any chance you want to call it off—"

"I don't." He cursed himself for the abrupt words he'd spoken two weeks ago that had made her believe he might not be in this for the long haul. "I love you, and we're getting married next spring."

Her lips trembled minutely. She sniffed delicately. He knew the stylist had taken a long time—over a half hour—to get her makeup just right. She wouldn't want to ruin it by crying.

He squeezed her hand again. "I'd kiss you if I weren't worried about messing up your lipstick. Your stylist is a little frightening. All those little metal tools..."

She smiled, like he'd hoped she would, the tense moment past.

They still had to find out who the thief was. There'd been some issue with the digital video, and the bank had had to request a backup copy. It was supposed to arrive first thing Monday morning.

Then there was going to be a reckoning on the ranch.

~ * ~

Ethan stood at the top of a secondary staircase in the huge mansion that someone called home. He'd arrived early enough to check in with the scary security dude at the front door—thank God Mia had gotten his name on the list—and to witness Mia announce the happy couple, who'd proceeded down the large main staircase like royalty—which Alessandra was—and then danced a complicated dance to the live violin and cello music playing from the center of the house.

From across the room, he'd only been able to catch a glimpse of Mia, who wore a powder-blue gown. Separated by probably a hundred and fifty guests in their fancy tuxedos and long dresses, he hadn't been able to get the crowd to part for him to make his way over to her. Then she'd disappeared completely.

So he'd climbed these stairs to see if he could spot her from above.

He'd checked his cell phone several times, in case

she was trying to locate him. Then he figured she might not have her phone on her with that fancy, frilly dress. Did something like that even have pockets?

One ugly whisper that sounded suspiciously like his stepmother's voice reverberated in his mind. *She doesn't really want you here.*

He tried his best to ignore the insidious voice, but it was difficult. Especially in light of his stepbrothers' actions from earlier in the day.

Then he spotted her. She moved effortlessly through the crowd, greeting those around her with the smile that never failed to make him week in the knees.

She looked up, caught sight of him. She was still halfway across the room, but he clearly saw the way her smile changed. Became more real somehow. A special smile, just for him.

He saw her lips form his name as she started toward the staircase.

Heart pounding in his ears, he made his way down the steps to meet her. The unfamiliar boots were a size too small and pinched his feet, but the cut of the borrowed tuxedo fit well, just enough room for his shoulders in the jacket.

He'd had to stop someone in the parking lot and get help with the bowtie.

But neither pinching shoes or tie issues mattered as he took in the light shining from Mia's eyes as she closed the last few feet between them.

Her dress was something else. The pale blue made

her skin luminescent, and she hadn't been joking when she'd mentioned the layer of fabric that he could easily see himself tripping on or stepping on if they really did try to dance. She was almost like a planet of her own.

He was definitely trapped in her gravitational field.

He stopped short, not wanting to muss her dress or the way her hair was perfectly styled, partly up and partly cascading down her back in soft curls.

She seemed to have no such compunction, because she threw herself the last two feet toward him, leaving him no choice but to catch her. He held her trim waist loosely between his hands, breathed in the sweet flowery perfume and just *Mia* beneath. Her huge skirt pressed against his legs, and he locked his limbs, afraid to move an inch and risk stepping on it.

He heard conversations cease nearby. Probably the who's who that was here wondered who he was to get a hug from the princess.

"You came," she whispered.

"You look... beautiful," he returned, his voice catching. This amazing creature counted him—*him!*—as a friend. Someone she wanted by her side. He still couldn't fathom it.

Her eyes shone at the compliment, and he was stunned all over again by her beauty. Inside and out.

"They're starting another waltz next," she said, "and I'd really like to dance with you."

"Are you sure?" he asked. "That might be a recipe for disaster."

She slid him a glance as she finally moved slightly

away from him. "I'm sure. Come on."

He followed her.

Couples had arranged themselves on the marble dance floor in one of the huge ballrooms. Mia's dress was definitely the widest, but he glanced side to side, taking in the countless floor-length skirts. There were a lot of people, especially considering they represented obstacles that he needed to watch out for.

The last thing he wanted to do was embarrass Mia by bumping into someone else or tripping her in that infernal skirt.

She seemed to read his mind as the musicians drew out a long note. "Keep it simple. Trust the music," she said softly, her chin tilting up. "I trust you."

And when she said something like that, he'd willingly throw himself off the cliff. The music started in earnest, and he followed the count. He found that if he kept to the small square that Mia had taught him and threw in a quarter turn every so often, it wasn't that hard.

He didn't step on her skirt. They didn't run into any of the other couples.

And he might be sweating through his undershirt, but having her smile up at him like he was worth something made him feel like he was flying.

~ * ~

With the happy couple busy greeting their guests and

the party going smoothly, Mia didn't want to waste another minute she could be spending with Ethan. After all, the palace had already scheduled her flight home for Monday morning.

So she dragged him out to the terrace, where a beautiful rose garden was putting out its final blooms of the season. She knew Gideon's security team had a presence out here, but they'd leave her and Ethan alone, if they knew what was good for them.

"That wasn't so bad, was it?" she teased. He'd done remarkably well with the simple waltz, and she'd been proud to be on his arm.

These past two weeks had been the happiest days of her life. Oh, there'd been bumps. She and Alessandra still hadn't patched things up, and she'd avoided two calls from Eloise.

But spending time with Ethan...discovering the kind of man he was...had been incredible.

She'd fallen for him. Hard. Her feelings were deeper than anything she'd experienced with anyone else.

He looked back to where the light spilled from the French doors that opened onto the terrace. Most of the partygoers remained inside, hoping to speak to Alessandra and Gideon, or to catch a glimpse of the other rich and famous guests, but some couples had meandered into the quiet darkness. Hopefully none of the invited press was out here, though she'd learned she could never be too careful.

"Are you sure you shouldn't be mingling? I don't want to keep you from your..." He made an uncertain gesture with one hand.

"Brad Pitt? I told you he declined the invite."

He smiled, but it faded too quickly. "I don't want to monopolize your time, if you're needed elsewhere."

And *that* was one of the reasons she'd fallen for him. Because he put her needs—and everyone else's—above his own.

"If you're worried about the duke and the soccer player," she said carefully, aware of what the tabloids had reported. "I said my *hellos* earlier. I would rather spend this time with you. I want to be with you." She finished with an honesty that would have been hard for her in the past.

Something intense flared in the depths of his eyes.

His selflessness was also why she hadn't spoken of the future. She wanted Ethan in her life, but she knew he was committed to raising his stepbrothers through their high school graduations. He'd told her some of his past, and people from town had been more than happy to fill in the rest. His stepmother's insistence that he devote all his spare time outside of schooling to maintaining the dairy. How *she* was the one who'd mishandled the property and sold it off to pay for her own extravagances.

Mia refused to add to his responsibilities or complicate his life. Surely, she could find reasons to visit the states—and Ethan—as often as possible. Which meant she needed to get over herself and talk to Alessandra and Eloise. Her sisters could smooth things over for her with travel plans and the international royal agenda.

But she also wanted tonight.

~ * ~

Ethan tried not to feel the magic of the night. He really did.

But he was already in love with Mia. And when she looked at him like that...

He knew that whatever was happening between them was just for tonight. It had to be.

He shifted his feet, his toes pinching.

"What's the matter?" Mia asked.

"Borrowed these boots." He shrugged. "Might have a blister in the morning, but it was worth it to dance with you."

She glowed in the moonlight. "We can do it again. Just take off your boots. No one will see your sock feet out here."

He made a face, but the boots were really starting to hurt, so he took them off and placed them on a nearby stone bench.

The music was low as it filtered through the open French doors.

And when she came into his arms, it wasn't in the waltz hold they'd practiced before. She was much closer. Both her arms came around his neck, leaving him to hold her waist between him hands. Beneath his palms, the material of her dress was soft and smooth.

He still couldn't fathom that she'd rather be out

here with him than inside with her old beaus.

"I've been thinking," she said. "That I'd like to stay in contact after all this."

She would?

She seemed to sense his incredulity, because she smiled softly up at him. "It won't be quite the same, but we can still talk on the phone. Send texts. And I'll be back in the states eventually."

He nodded, stunned and running her words through his mind. She wanted to continue their friendship.

He knew that eventually she'd be distracted by her royal life. Or the man she'd eventually fell in love with.

Just thinking about that gave him heartburn.

And then suddenly his jacket pocket was buzzing. Or rather, his phone.

He ignored it, focusing on Mia's dear face, trying to soak her in for the long days when she was gone.

But it rang again, and she moved slightly back, letting go. "It might be important."

When the screen lit, he saw it was straight up midnight. He didn't recognize the number. He connected the call.

"This is the county sheriff," the voice on the line said. "I've got your brothers in custody. They're drunk. We picked them up for breaking into the feed store in town. They did quite a bit of damage."

He couldn't find words.

Mia watched him from too close, and he turned his back to her, not wanting her to overhear, to be tainted by his family drama. He knew there was press attending the event tonight, and knew that Mia wanted to stay out of the limelight.

Finally, he got his voice to work, though it was rough. "I'll be there as soon as I can."

He still couldn't think straight as he turned back to Mia. She wore a concerned expression and reached out one hand to him, but he pulled back before she could touch him.

"I have to go," he said, the words wooden. His stepbrothers had ruined this night not once, but twice.

"Ethan, can I help you—?"

He shook his head violently, not wanting her to become a part of this. "I just—I have to go."

He gathered his boots from the bench, not bothering to put them on. Urgency surged through him. His stepbrothers were in jail.

Mia was close behind him, wanting to help, but he couldn't face her right now.

Before she could stop him, before she could say something that would make everything hurt worse, he walked off, brushing past a buff guy in a suit who had to be security. Ethan rounded the house instead of going inside, hitting the parking lot and then his truck in his sock feet. He tossed the boots to the floorboard and cranked the engine.

His brothers had ruined his night, but that wasn't the worst of it.

What if they'd ruined their chances for a new future?

What did that mean for *Ethan's* future?

CHAPTER SEVEN

At seven the next morning, Ethan sat in the county judge's chambers. His elbows rested on his knees, and he stared at his feet. It was Saturday, so the courthouse was empty and quiet, but the judge had made an emergency exception and allowed Ethan to come in so he could plead on his stepbrothers' behalf.

He hadn't slept all night. He'd started at the county sheriff's office, where they'd told him the judge wouldn't be in until Monday. He'd gone home to make phone calls and change out of the borrowed tuxedo, only then realizing he was missing one of the fancy black dress boots. Which meant he'd have to go back to the mansion where the ball had been held and find it later. And if he didn't, then maybe he'd have to call Mia, if the book wasn't lying in the gardens or parking lot.

He hadn't slept at all. Had stayed awake praying and worrying and trying to figure out a way to get his stepbrothers out of this mess.

Apparently, the idiots had gotten drunk with some of their friends and decided it would be fun to ride the tractor mowers parked in front of the feed store. He couldn't imagine where they'd gotten the keys. But they'd turned on at least one mower and driven it through the front windows of the store, destroying thousands of dollars' worth of merchandise.

He didn't know if he could fix this. There was no money in the budget to retain an attorney. How would the boys even make restitution? What would this do for their college plans? School?

"Back again, young man?" The judge, in his fifties with a balding head and hard-to-read eyes, entered the room. His long black robe flowed around him as he moved to sit behind a huge, old-looking wooden desk.

"Hello, your honor." Ethan had hoped never to see him again after last summer when the boys had been charged with vandalism.

The judge shuffled some papers on his desk and flipped open a manila folder. He didn't speak to Ethan again as he read whatever was in that document.

"Your brothers—excuse me, your stepbrothers— appear to be in a mess of trouble. We talked last summer about them getting a second chance, but it sure seems as if they've squandered it."

Ethan nodded miserably. "I'm really sorry, sir. They'd been a little more responsible since last summer..." He let the words trail off, because what they'd done last night obviously belied the statement. He glanced at the door behind him. "Shouldn't they be in here?"

The judge flipped the folder closed and leaned back in his chair, which protested with a metallic squeak. "I wanted to talk with you first, before I see your stepbrothers."

Ethan's stomach tightened into a little ball of misery. This didn't sound good.

"They were what, ten and eleven when you were granted custody of them?"

"Yes, sir." Ethan wiped sweaty palms on his jean-clad thighs.

"Did you know that last summer, after their arrest, I got several phone calls and two letters from your neighbors and friends?"

What? That was news to Ethan. "No, sir."

"They all wanted me to know how much you were sacrificing for those boys and how you'd tried your best not only to provide for them, but to teach them how to be good citizens."

He had tried to impart the lessons Dad had taught him, but somehow it'd gone all wrong. He didn't know how, couldn't see where he'd missed a crucial element, but clearly he had, because Robbie and Sam didn't get it. Ethan rubbed the bridge of his nose, behind which an ache built that he couldn't seem to get rid of.

"You've got good friends," the judge said.

Ethan nodded dumbly. He knew it. Just like the vet who'd watched out for him yesterday evening. But what did that have to do with his stepbrothers?

"And you've done your best to influence those boys. But I've been doing this a long time, and do you know what I see?"

The question didn't seem to require an answer. Ethan kept quiet.

"I see two young men who've been given every chance. Been taught right from wrong. Been loved on. And they still make bad choices. It's not your fault," the judge said quickly when Ethan squeezed his eyes shut. "You've given six years of your life to caring for and providing for these boys."

Longer, if one counted the time he'd spend working for his stepmother before his eighteenth birthday.

"It's my decision that your influence alone, as good as it's been, isn't enough to keep those two on the straight and narrow. They are removed from your custody and will become wards of the state. They'll likely have to serve some time in a youth detention facility for what they've done. They're not first-time offenders. And they're old enough to know better."

He sat dumbly in the chair. Not knowing what to feel. He would no longer have charge of his stepbrothers. He'd failed them.

Or they'd failed themselves.

His mind whirled with hurt, despair, fears for his stepbrothers.

He stood up, not sure what he should say. *Thank you* didn't seem quite right.

The older man stood too, then rounded his desk before clapping a hand on Ethan's shoulder. "This isn't your fault. You understand?"

How could it not be? When Ethan was supposed

to have taught Robbie and Sam right from wrong?

"A lot of people care about you—as evidenced by their phone calls and letters from last summer. You've done your best. But your stepbrothers haven't. That's all this is."

Ethan walked out of the office feeling sick to his stomach. He didn't know where to turn. Whether he should try to see his stepbrothers and say goodbye.

The last time he'd spoken to them, Robbie had thrown Ethan's actions in his face. They'd destroyed his dad's suit, one of his few reminders of his father. He could still see his dad in that suit—wore it to church every Sunday.

But Robbie and Sam—they'd been ungrateful and rude.

Would saying goodbye provide closure or just pour gasoline on the fire of his stepbrothers' hatred?

~ * ~

Monday morning, Gideon had wanted to come to the bank by himself, but Alessandra had parked herself in the passenger seat of his truck with arms crossed and refused to move.

So here they were, seated side-by-side at a desk in the manager's office, with the county sheriff behind them as digital video played over a large computer monitor.

The bank manager stood nervously behind Gideon's shoulder. Gideon knew the man was worried about liability being placed on his bank or his employees, but as far as Gideon was concerned, whoever had perpetrated this theft was to blame. Not the bank.

"The time stamp was for 10:50 a.m.," the bank manager said nervously.

The video feed on the computer monitor showed that the digital film was approaching that time, and Gideon found himself squinting at the screen, waiting to see a grainy image of Nate cross into the footage.

But when it came, it wasn't Nate.

"That's Dan," Alessandra whispered.

It sure was. The ball cap pulled low over his face wasn't enough to shield him from the cameras, and they watched as the cowhand presented a piece of paper to the cashier. They watched as ten grand was counted out to him by the bank teller.

A half hour later, Dan sat with head in hands in the Triple H dining room. The sheriff read him his rights, and he sat silently, unmoving.

Dan didn't fight the arrest, though Gideon stood nearby as backup, just in case. The sheriff was armed, though, and Dan seemed more resigned than anything else. Nate had followed them up from the barn and stood in the doorway, watching in horror.

When the sheriff had finished, he looked to Gideon, maybe silently asking whether he wanted to confront the man or not.

But it was Nate who burst out with a question.

"If you needed money, why didn't you come to me?" Nate's words emerged angry, but Gideon knew his foreman must feel the same betrayal and hurt beneath that Gideon did.

Dan shook his head, not raising his gaze from the table. "You'd already bailed me out once, man."

That was news to Gideon, who cut his gaze to the foreman.

Nate ignored him, his entire focus on Dan. "So you just *stole* it? Stole from Gideon, who gave you a job outta high school, when you had nowhere else to turn?"

He sounded like he wanted to smack the other man upside the head, but Gideon shook his head in warning as the sheriff ushered Dan out of the room.

Alessandra perched at the long table as if all the air had been sucked out of her entire body. Gideon reached for her, and she met his hand, linking their fingers together. "Now we know," she said.

"Yeah." It didn't quite cure the bitter taste that had been lingering in the back of his throat these past weeks. But at least they could close the case. Move forward, if he could figure out how to do that now.

"Any reason you didn't tell me about missing *ten grand*?" Nate asked, drawing Gideon's gaze away from his woman.

Nate stood with feet spread and arms crossed, looking like he wanted to do battle. He stared at Gideon for a long moment before realization dawned on his face. "You thought *I* took it?"

Guilt flushed into Gideon's face, but he didn't back down. "I thought whoever had the easiest access to the bank account and the computerized ledgers did it. I'm sorry." He was man enough to apologize when he'd been so very, very wrong.

Nate took off his Stetson and slapped it against his thigh, sending a little puff of dust flying from his jeans. "I've been with you for ten years, man. How could you think I'd steal from you?"

Alessandra started to speak up, but Gideon cut her off with a wave of his hand. This was his mess to deal with. "You want to tell me why you loaned Dan a chunk of cash to pay off his...what, gambling debts?"

He must've hit right on the money, because Nate flushed a dull red through his neck and jaw.

"You knew one of the hands had a problem and didn't tell me?" Gideon pressed.

Nate's lips firmed into a white line.

Gideon didn't want to fight and he didn't want to lose their friendship. He purposely relaxed his stance, let his arms hang loose at his sides. "It seems like we both made mistakes." He let that sink in for a moment. "You know I don't trust easy."

Nate snorted, but his frown relaxed slightly.

"Understatement," Alessandra whispered.

Gideon cut a glance at her to let her know she'd pay for that dig later.

"This whole situation," Gideon circled his hand between the three of them. "Me being gone, laying more on your shoulders, *trusting you more*. It's going to take some getting used to. For all of us," he said with an eye-squint at Alessandra. "So we didn't get it right on the first try. The Triple H needs you. I need you."

The words weren't easy for Gideon to say. Alessandra squeezed his hand in support.

Nate's frown disappeared almost completely. "We might not be blood, but we're family." He stuck out his hand.

Gideon shook it.

LACY WILLIAMS

CHAPTER EIGHT

On Sunday, Mia had tagged along with Gideon and Alessandra to their small church. She'd been enjoying a cup of coffee in the lobby when she'd overheard two women discussing Ethan and what had happened to his brothers over the weekend.

That afternoon, she hadn't wasted any time in enlisting Alessandra's help and making an impromptu video call to Eloise.

Now Monday morning, the sun was rising, and she was camped out on Ethan's back porch, waiting for him to come in from milking the cows.

Even though his world might be imploding, she knew he wouldn't be shirking his responsibilities.

Hearing secondhand about what he'd been through over the weekend, she'd realized he'd pushed her away the night of the ball at least partly because he'd known there was press in attendance and even more camped out in the parking lot. If she'd run off with him to the county jail, they'd have had a field day.

He'd wanted to protect her.

She wasn't *falling* in love with him. She *loved* him.

Real love. True love.

The kind of love that made sacrifices. The kind of love she'd been waiting for all her life.

She wasn't waiting any longer.

She was going to be here for Ethan, for as long as he needed her. Hopefully for life.

There was a rush of cows exiting the back of the barn into the pasture. Then, a few minutes later, Ethan emerged from the front of the barn. He had his head down, and his shoulders were low, as if he carried a weight too heavy to bear.

She was ready to come beside him and bear some of it, too.

He must've sensed her presence, because his head came up as he entered the backyard gate. He stood stock still for a moment, staring at her. Peanut had had her head snuggled into Mia's lap, but she raised her chin and gave one happy bark to welcome him. The dog's tail thumped on the wood deck.

Ethan turned to carefully latch the gate closed. He took off his gloves as he approached, stopping at the bottom of the stairs. Too far away for Mia's purposes.

"Hey."

~ * ~

"Hey."

Ethan couldn't stop staring at Mia. Part of him was sure this was a dream, that he'd missed his three-thirty alarm and was fantasizing the entire thing.

She stood up, dislodging his dog and straightening to reveal the worn jeans and flannel shirt she had on. He'd never seen her in something so casual. She was even wearing worn-out boots.

Had he conjured up his perfect fantasy? A Mia who was his to keep?

"Seems you dropped this when you rushed out of the ball the other night." She held up something black. The dress boot he'd been missing.

He took it from her, the leather cool against his fingers.

He cleared his throat. "I thought you'd be packing for your flight."

An awful ache spread through him, just saying the words. He'd tried not to think about it all weekend, the fact that she was leaving. That he'd probably never see her again, even though she'd said otherwise the other night.

She moved down one step, which still put her a head above him. Two porch steps still separated them. "I made up with Alessandra."

He nodded, not sure what that had to do with her leaving.

"Turns out that family is one of the more important things in life, and between the both of us, we decided not to let our father's secrets and lies ruin our relationship."

He was glad for her. But the wounds his stepbrothers had inflicted over the weekend hadn't even formed a scab yet, and he felt a great gaping hole where he'd failed them.

Mia descended another stair, but in his hurt, he couldn't look at her. Instead, he averted his gaze over her shoulder.

"Alessandra also helped facilitate a conversation with my older sister." She descended the final step, which put her close enough to touch, though he didn't. "Basically, I told them both that I'm not leaving Texas."

At her words, his gaze flew to her face. "What?" *She wasn't leaving?*

She didn't answer with words. Instead, her arms came around his neck, and she stood on tiptoe as she leaned into him.

His hand that wasn't holding the borrowed boot came around her waist by reflex.

This time, she didn't give him room to question whether he was imagining her intent. She slid her hands into the hair at the nape of his neck and gave a gentle tug, bringing his head down.

She kissed him.

There was no room for thought as her lips feathered over his. She pressed in closer, and he dropped the boot, which fell with a soft *thunk*. His other hand slid around her waist.

He hadn't kissed anyone since Sarah Myers in the fifth grade, and this was nothing like that.

He moved wrong, and their chins bumped, breaking the kiss. But Mia only smiled and reached up to kiss him again. Her lips were incredibly soft, and she tasted like coffee and mint, and he never wanted to stop kissing her.

But of course, they eventually had to stop to catch their breath.

She didn't let go of him, and he was no fool. He pressed her close to his thudding heart, mind and adrenaline racing.

"Mia?"

She hummed from where she was tucked against his chest.

He didn't know quite how to get the question out. "You said—you said that the next time you kissed someone, it was going to be the man you wanted to marry." Okay, that wasn't a question at all, but who could think after those passionate kisses?

She didn't tease him. She moved slightly away, just enough that she could tilt her face up and see his.

He felt vulnerable even putting the suggestion out there. It seemed ludicrous. That someone like *her* would want to marry someone like *him*.

She reached up with one hand to cup his jaw. "I think you can safely consider that kiss my proposal."

Her *proposal.*

A hot burn started behind his nose. He had to be sure. "You want to marry *me?*"

She nodded, her eyes taking on a shine that might be happiness or might be tears.

He squeezed her close again, burying his face in her hair just in case some of the emotion overwhelming him snuck out as tears.

He didn't even realize he was shaking until he felt her hands brush calming strokes down his back. Never in a million years had he imagined this happening.

After she'd kissed him again, just to make sure he understood exactly what she was proposing, they sat side-by-side on the top step with their hands linked and her head on his shoulder.

Somehow she'd found out about his custody issue. Or non-issue. "If you want to fight for custody of your stepbrothers, the palace can help with obtaining the best attorneys."

He exhaled. And finally admitted to some of what had been running through his head all weekend. Or maybe for weeks, since he'd met with the principal. "It feels wrong to say this, but...maybe it's time to let them go. Robbie and Sam don't want to be with me. They've proved that over and over."

It felt a little like giving up, but with Mia looking at him like he hung the stars, it soothed the wound somewhat.

She reached up and bussed his cheek with a kiss, leaving a cinnamon-burn sensation behind as she nestled back against his shoulder. "So what do you want to do? Rebuild your dad's legacy here? Or...there *are* universities in Glorvaird. I know we could find the best veterinary program for you there."

Possibilities stretched before him. Limitless, with Mia at his side. He didn't even know what to think, what to start dreaming about first.

He had the best dream, the brightest star, right here with him.

She seemed to understand, because she grinned up

at him, a smile both mischievous and light. "You don't have to decide right now."

And she kissed him again.

LACY WILLIAMS

EPILOGUE

One week later

"Are you sure you really want to do this?" Alessandra's teasing question turned Mia's head from where she'd been staring at the flower-adorned front of the small Las Vegas wedding chapel.

But her sister wasn't asking her. She was asking Ethan, who stood tall and handsome at Mia's side in his borrowed tux—and the new pair of dress boots she'd made him purchase to wear with it.

"Mia is notoriously grumpy in the mornings," Alessandra went on. "And you don't even want to know about her shopping habits."

Ethan looked to Mia, and his gaze didn't waver. "I'm sure I'll never find another woman as special as Mia."

Her heart thudded, and she shared a quick glance with Alessandra that expressed *aw!*

From slightly behind and to one side of her sister, Gideon made a face. Mia forgave him for it, because she knew he could be just as romantic as Ethan— after all, she'd overheard his romantic sentiments to her sister even before she'd met the man.

"I'm a little less certain that this is the kind of wedding Mia deserves," Ethan said.

Mia slipped her hand into his, edging closer. "We could do a fancy wedding in Glorvaird with five hundred in attendance—people you don't know and who'd only be there to be seen. It would take months to plan, and there'd be a million little details."

Over Alessandra's shoulder, Gideon groaned.

Mia didn't look away from Ethan's face. "But I don't want to wait."

His gaze crackled with intensity, and he smiled a slow smile. "I don't want to wait, either. If you're sure."

She was.

With Alessandra on her side, she'd talked to Eloise at length about Ethan's situation. She technically didn't need permission to get married, but she also didn't want to make things more difficult with father, considering he might not be with them for much longer.

Finally, her sister had agreed that because of the media storm that always followed Mia around, a Vegas wedding wouldn't do irreparable harm to the royal family's reputation or diplomatic connections.

Ethan had made peace with losing custody of his brothers, though Mia knew he still felt guilty, as if he'd let them down—which she found ridiculous. She kept that opinion to herself.

After much thought and prayer, Ethan had decided that while the dairy farm was his dad's legacy, it wasn't his dream to rebuild. They'd already begun looking for a buyer. Once the transaction closed, they would relocate—with Peanut—to Glorvaird.

Mia knew Ethan would make a fine prince. His finer qualities, his loyalty and goodness, would win over the hearts of her people, just as he'd won her over.

She couldn't wait to take him home. But first...

The rented minister beckoned them to the front of the small chapel. Gideon, who wore a suit, and Alessandra, who wore a simple wine-colored shift, walked arm-in-arm down the aisle first, leaving Mia and Ethan to follow.

She'd chosen an off-the-shoulder floor-length satin sheath and held a simple bouquet of roses in a deep red that matched Alessandra's dress.

She could see what Ethan thought of her in his eyes as he looked at her as if he couldn't tear his gaze away.

There was no doubt in her mind that this was right. Ethan was her one true love, and she knew they'd be blissfully happy together. For life.

~ * ~

"They look happy," Gideon whispered in Alessandra's ear as they witnessed Mia and Ethan speak their vows. They'd foregone the typical maid of honor and best man placement to stand together near the bride and groom.

And Ethan and Mia did look happy. He hadn't known Mia well before this trip—still didn't consider himself close with her—but Alessandra had expressed several times that she'd never seen her sister more settled and at peace.

Love did that for you.

For those few tense days when he'd been in the midst of investigating the Triple H theft, he'd questioned whether his and Alessandra's love would be enough to hold them together. When he should've been holding on to her. After the dust up with Dan, he and Nate had sat down and worked out some security measures for the ranch's finances and worked through some of the communication issues they'd had when Gideon had been gone to Glorvaird for weeks on end.

He hoped they could still make the transition work, for both his and Alessandra's sake, and for the Triple H.

There was still the issue of the royal family's overall security. Although nothing had happened in several months, and the threats they had received had been garden-variety and harmless, he wasn't convinced that the threat was over. If Alessandra's aunt was truly unhinged, danger could lurk around the next bend.

And he'd just gotten an email this morning from one of his contacts regarding Alessandra and Mia's half-sister. His guy had found a last known alias and an address. The information was several years old. It wasn't much to go on, but it was better than the nothing he'd had before.

Alessandra had been sequestered with her sister in

their shared hotel room all morning, so Gideon hadn't had a chance to tell her yet. He could only hope this led to something positive.

What if the missing half-sister wasn't what Alessandra was building her up in her mind to be?

He wouldn't let his girl get hurt, but how did he protect her from this family issue that had been years in the making, since Alessandra had been a little girl?

All he could do was be there for her.

She glanced over her shoulder at him, eyes moist and shiny.

He leaned slightly closer, so he could whisper to her again. "Do we really have to invite five hundred people to ours?"

Her smile widened.

He'd go through the circus act of a big wedding. Heck, he'd walk through fire if she would just keep smiling at him like that, for the rest of their lives.

~ * ~

Pieter might technically be a prince, but he'd never met his royal cousins. The crown princess and her two sisters lived in the royal palace in the heart of Glorvaird, while Pieter, his mother, and his older brother Henri had been forced out of the kingdom. They resided in a villa in nearby Regis, a small territory close to Glorvaird.

It was a comfortable living, at least financially. The king of Glorvaird had been unable to sever his mother's inheritance, though he'd done everything in his power to ruin their lives.

Pieter and Henri had been dealing with their mother's eccentricities alone, ever since they'd been young boys.

But lately, things had grown worse.

Pieter had one love—bicycle racing. He wasn't good enough to ride in the Tour de France, but he'd hired on as a driver to follow and assist the team. In the weeks he'd been absent, apparently his mother had hired assassins in some hare-brained attempt that made sense only to her to claim the crown. Henri had gone incommunicado. Disappeared.

His mother's plot had been a mess to clean up and had cost more to keep quiet than he'd like to think about.

He was tired. Tired of dealing with his mom's mental health problems on his own. Tired of being rejected by a country that was in his blood.

He wanted to be acknowledged by the royal family. And a small part of him wanted to hurt them like he'd been hurt by the abandonment he'd suffered his whole life.

He just had to discover the best way to enact revenge.

It wasn't hard to follow his cousins' movements via the American media. Except for Eloise, who never seemed to leave the palace.

Could he insert himself in his cousins' life, without revealing his true identity? He'd need to be close to find out what could truly cause them pain.

After all, he'd learned from his mother, the master of pain.

LACY WILLIAMS

ABOUT THE AUTHOR

USA Today bestselling author Lacy Williams works in a hostile environment (read: four kids age 7 and under). In spite of this, she has somehow managed to be a hybrid author since 2011, publishing 34 books & novellas. Lacy's books have finaled in the *RT Book Reviews* Reviewers' Choice Awards (2012, 2013, & 2014), the Golden Quill and the Booksellers Best Award. She is a member of American Christian Fiction Writers, Romance Writers of America and Novelists Inc.

Made in the USA
Middletown, DE
22 September 2021

48831358R00182